The Armor of Ancient Ghosts

By: Philip A. Kay

*I dedicate this tale to my late
father,
Dr. Mario C. Kay
Long live Sparta! Long live Hellas!
Philip A. Kay*

Introduction

King Leonidas

Late summer, a swelteringly hot day in central Greece. Vultures by the hundreds circled, ominously casting a morphing shadow over the horrific landscape of the dead and still-dying. They were enticed here by the thousands of deceased soldiers deteriorating on this cruel battlefield. The large scavengers scanned the vast uneven ground looking for a meal, occasionally descending and gorging themselves on the dead until getting spooked and retreating.

So many lifeless bodies were stacked obscenely upon one another in this now oddly muted landscape. The men lay randomly positioned in their final agonizing moments. They resembled pale, bloody statues that told a grim story of defiance, leaking their remaining fluids into the coagulating mud bog on which they now lay silently.

Their honor was the one thing that remained intact, and it was now feeding this cursed piece of stained earth with the righteous paroxysms of their begotten souls in ascension. The Spartans and Greeks, who fought so valiantly, resisted the onslaught until the last man finally succumbed to the sheer volume of the invading army's colossal mass.

However, the men defending their homelands held out, only finally collapsing in a "still" proud defeat. Though the Persian forces had won the day, they were not jubilantly celebrating a clear and decisive victory. They perished in alarming numbers, at a rate of almost fifteen to one against the combined Spartan and Hellenic force.

The Spartan commander, King Leonidas, sacrificed himself and his brave soldiers to afford the populations of Sparta and Athens time to seek shelter from the dark, lumbering shadow of the inevitable Persian invasion. Wave after battering wave of Persian shock troops came to the skirmish line to test their mettle against King Leonidas and his battle-hardened men, only to be bluntly repelled repeatedly to the billowing dismay of the many echelons of Persian commanders.

Finally, after many thwarted attempts, Xerxes' high command gained new intelligence about a goat trail they could exploit. It led to a location where they could outflank the Greeks, who maintained a shrewd defense in a narrow rocky corridor. Despite knowing of this Achilles' heel, Leonidas held fast; he was only buying time with his and his men's lives to allow secret evacuations to proceed unimpeded, enabling the Greeks to fight another day. They held on for three arduous days of unceasing hand-to-hand combat before finally collapsing under the overwhelming tide of the Persian onslaught. After the dust of the battle settled and the last arrow spiraled through the air, piercing its final victim, the Spartan resistance lay decimated by Xerxes' enormous assault.

This hallowed ground is where our story begins …

Chapter 1

Dreams of Ghosts

Whips snapped and echoed off the sheer cliff walls; Persian slaves descended upon the narrow strait and began the nauseating process of searching for the still-living soldiers among the countless dead. Wagons groaned and creaked, pulled by oxen as they came and left the gruesome scene loaded down with the wretched remains of so many brave warriors.

They didn't even resemble human beings anymore; instead, they were armless, legless, headless creatures, covered in dirt, sculpted into horrific unreal forms. Their frozen faces showed the extreme torment brought on by this perverse and ancient brand of human suffering, one that usually only rears its ugly head when autocratic tyrants desire to expand their territories.

These deranged sociopathic leaders, infected with false piety and nefarious ambitions, impose unspeakable violence on their foes to embezzle more power and control. They are incited by political sycophants, middlemen who quietly inflate their regent's maniacal egos in the shadows, constantly creatively leveraging their appointment for their own ill-gotten gain. They levy heavy-handed governance as a vehicle of acute social order and an indicator of prosperity, but only by inflicting terror into the hearts of the very same people they wish to reign over. This perversion of power spared none.

The brave Spartan warriors lay in a small pocket in the center amid this swelling carnage. They held together in formation until the last of the men collapsed under the sheer mass of the final Persian assault. They fought selflessly and bravely, these Spartan warriors and Greek militia. Some of the fallen Spartan warriors even bore menacing pale blue smiles on their stiffened lips, almost as if rewarded for their toil and sacrifice with an honorable warrior's death. They now assumed a seat at the table of their warrior ancestors as the sparse bits of oxygen dissipated in their last expiring heartbeats.

The Persian stretcher-bearers and their slaves thought this such a queer last expression for the dead to have molded on their faces after gruesomely dying in battle. It was as if the Spartans had perversely enjoyed the release from their mortal existence, which terrified the slaves. The frightened men kicked dirt onto the smiling faces to cover up the blue-lipped sarcasm that only seemed to mock their hideously morbid task on this day.

As the servants combed through these mounds of wasted humanity, they lifted a corpse and uncovered a Spartan soldier they had previously assumed dead. The man suddenly gasped a deep, heaving breath and started raising his hand into the thick air, trembling as if grasping at some unreachable terminus just beyond the radiating sky above. The slaves were a highly superstitious lot, frightened out of their wits by the surprise motion of one of the soldiers they previously thought deceased. They proclaimed excitedly, all clamoring "This must be black magic!" as they began running away from where the Greek "ghost" soldier seemed to return to haunt them from beyond the grave.

As the slaves rapidly abandoned the area in fear and complete disarray, the Persian physician Alborz Amani performed mercy killings on the mortally wounded, and overheard the men's frantic and incoherent ravings. They were apologizing to the gods, declaring some nonsense of wronging the smiling "ghost" warrior too soon before his departure into the afterlife. They feared they had enticed the man's spirit back from the dead to haunt them; angering and disturbing his last bloody moments would have far-reaching consequences.

The doctor stood before the exodus of slaves, holding up his hands to get the procession to stop and tell him why they were leaving their work unfinished. He listened to one slave's howling descriptions of a man still moving in such an injured state that he could not believe his own eyes. An older, less agitated slave stopped him and told him he had retrieved many dead men on Persian battlefields but never one injured to this extent. The doctor thought a man surviving such mortal injuries would be a prize to his superiors. Amani scanned the battlefield to find this "so-called" Spartan ghost.

He approached the edge of the sprawl the slaves abandoned, spotting the fallen warrior. He cautiously approached him, seeing a slight contrast in the color of his skin from the other bodies around him. A wound on his arm was still rhythmically pumping small amounts of blood from a vein, a sign of a still-beating heart. He crouched down and attempted to give the wounded Spartan medical aid. This brave soldier had multiple arrows protruding from his torso, and deep lacerations and contusions from sword, spear, and beast, plainly apparent all over his battered body. The fallen soldier opened his eyes; he stared scornfully at the physician through the dust and blood encrusted on his face.

The doctor could see down to the bone in some of the man's wounds, but the soldier just stared at Amani with an evil eye of defiance before his body slumped limp and unconscious back onto the bloody soil again. The physician immediately wrapped the man's wounds tightly in dry cloths to stop his bleeding. He called his colleagues and a few other slaves to help him carefully evacuate the man to the triage camp for further evaluation. Xerxes' physicians were at the top of their caste in Persian society and regarded almost at the same level as priests or military commanders. Both commoners and royalty alike held the physicians in the highest regard. At festivals, the people exulted them to an almost celebrity status due to their intelligence and wise understanding of life and the human form, both inside and out. They felt they deserved this sensational adulation because of the honors Xerxes bestowed upon them in public. At many formal ceremonial pageants, the physicians would sit on high in the observation stands next to the Persian commanders who welcomed them for their clinical expertise on their battlefields. The commanders applauded the efforts of these educated men to repair and heal the badly injured soldiers. Many of the commanders had witnessed some of the most gruesome injuries up close and firsthand while fighting to fulfill their king's sometimes insane whims. The type of trauma from this manner of warfare and the damage it inflicted on the human body fascinated the physicians. For all the commanders could imagine, their lives might be saved if the tide of a battle didn't swing their way one day.

These physicians, though Persian, had taken the same solemn oath to the gods not to harm, the same as the Greek physicians. Although they viewed this oath a little differently than the Western doctors, to them, wounded prisoners of war were still the enemy and the best subjects on which to experiment, testing and honing their skills of tissue and bone reconstruction unimpeded.

They forged new methods of surgery and triage on the wounded men without the fear of any shred of negative oversight. They rejoiced in all the opportunities and possibilities of repairing some of the broken and disfigured human bodies that Xerxes' armies regularly produced for them. Some poor soldiers they resurrected from the wounded enemy's ranks should have been left to die gracefully.

Instead, Xerxes' twisted perversions spurred on and invigorated this cruel practice of rescue and reanimation. He celebrated the genuinely bizarre and amazingly reconstructed human form, and demanded that the surgeons keep creating these prototype humans with missing appendages and freakish disfigurements to add to his growing collection. This procurement was simply for his entertainment, always satisfying his grotesque and perverse fascination with these poor souls.

For what seemed like an eternity, the slaves kept piling the stiffened soldiers' corpses on wagons, occasionally extricating a man still barely clinging to life. They pulled the still-moving aside for evacuation. They stacked the casualties on ox carts, withdrew from the battlefield, and dumped the expired bodies on an enormous pyre. Smoke billowed high in the air as they immolated the dead. The gods thirsted for these human offerings and demanded powerful men's souls to fill their ranks in the afterlife, and so the process trudged on long into the darkness of night.

At the conclusion of this morose event, the slaves had recovered three barely living Spartan soldiers and fifty-one wounded Greek soldiers. They found most barely breathing but still occupying the thin precipice between wounded and dead. Heroic warrior martyrs, so very close to their ultimate glory, but now mightily plucked from death's final bequest.

The three Spartan warriors retrieved this day were so gravely wounded that they could not resist any treatment given to them by the Persian field medics. These physicians could instantly tell the Greek and Spartan survivors apart ... Spartans looked like statues, like chiseled, muscled beasts, with flowing long hair adorned in scarlet sashes.

The ordinary Greek soldiers were just a little-above-average-sized men, trained skilled laborers, and wealthy landowners who were ultimately defending their families and properties. The men were separated from the rest of the soldiers, loaded onto the wagons, and immediately taken to the field triage camp at the rear of the Persian advance.

Once there, the men's wounds were to be correctly cleaned and dressed personally by Xerxes' royal physicians. They saved these men's lives only so they could boast to their superiors about the rare find, hopefully finding higher favor in the Persian ranks. Not once in this generation could they remember a Spartan soldier being captured alive … Back in the time of Hystaspes, there were no such victories; only dead Spartans showed themselves to their enemy in person if a battle were lost.

Upon hearing of these barely breathing soldiers being retrieved from the bleeding grounds of Thermopylae, Xerxes immediately proceeded to the triage tents to speak with his laboring physicians and view his new human prizes. Xerxes rarely visited the front line. He only showed up to understand how many of his men had "not" shown true courage and fought unto the death, willfully surviving to dishonor his name in battle rather than fighting valiantly to a futile and bitter end. On some occasions, Xerxes would single out a man with very few injuries and run him through with his dagger to project his utter disdain for cowardice on the battlefield; it was a warning to the half-hearted soldiers who were not wholly dedicated to victory; it was a statement to the rest to do as they were instructed or else face his violent wrath.

After arriving at the medical tents, he was quickly taken aside and briefed by his royal handlers; they explained that three Spartan soldiers were captured and, in the physicians' custody. These men were unconscious, bruised, and their flesh badly lacerated, but still, they clung to life by a sheer unconscious will to exist. Xerxes, who rarely smiled or displayed emotion in public, was beyond elated. He paced, wringing his hands, and sternly warned his physicians, *if the Spartans die in your care, you too will suffer this fate, and be it by my hand; this is my will! I will have my pets breathing and interred in plush cages!*

Xerxes' head physician, Menna Al Farouk, gulped and swallowed the thick saliva in his dry, parched throat, now sweating in nervous disbelief. He pleaded carefully with Xerxes to reconsider this lofty royal mandate, noting the extreme condition of the three wounded men. He exclaimed, "Xerxes, my honorable regent; these men are on a thin edge of being, in a precarious state much closer to death's embrace than to life's vague promise." He warned King Xerxes, "Their mere survival, in this case, is not guaranteed. In fact, we have never seen living bodies so incredibly mangled yet warm with blood still pulsing through their constricted hearts!"

He surmised they would probably not make it through the night no matter how much care was given. Before this moment, only the corpses they had encountered and dissected had such extraordinary wounds. "These men's injuries are so gruesome, they test our abilities even to control their bleeding!"

Xerxes just looked down at Al Farouk disapprovingly, shaking his head, and began walking away with an air of disgust in his dark brown eyes. He scoffed at the incessant groveling of this so-called "educated man."

"Upon my return to the palace, I wish to see my pets treated well and in cages; you will do this for me, or you will pay dearly with your head on a stick for all to see! Would your wife and children be pleased to see you in this way, Dr. Al Farouk ...? I think not. Now, do as you are told!"

Seeing the immense gravity of his now dire situation, Dr. Al Farouk apologized for his insolence, bowing repeatedly as the king exited the tent.

A shaken Al Farouk decided to stay with the convalescing soldiers both night and day until they were stable enough to be moved by cart to a more clean and civilized setting.

Al Farouk pulled back the flesh from around one of the Spartan's left thighs, exposing the bone that had been hacked with a sword or axe strike. He washed tiny fragments of bone, dirt, and clothing threads from the gaping gash. It was almost a surgically clean cut from a sharp blade that had lacerated the flesh. Another soldier had collapsed on top of this man's wound, ultimately and inadvertently applying pressure to the gaping cut by the weight of his folded body, which kept the Spartan from bleeding out.

The doctor looked closely at the bone, which was almost entirely severed in half. Once Al Farouk had removed all the debris from the gaping cavity, he flushed it with a Rakki and saltwater solution. He then inspected it closely for puss and signs of morbidity. Only a few veins had been severed, and no real taring had occurred. He began the slow, arduous process of putting the muscles back together with a needle and a fine silk thread, then splinted and wrapped the wounded area in alcohol-soaked cloths. He aligned the veins and used a small hot piece of bronze he had created to sear the walls of the vessels together. He had learned the power of glowing hot metal to seal wounds on previous battlefields. He reasoned that it should also work internally if it worked outside the body.

Al Farouk had also learned the trick of using the strong grain wine from his medical teachers in Persepolis. They did not understand why, but they knew that when you used the spirits to clean wounds, the patients recovered without having the wound become putrid and going through the amputation of the limb or having to apply maggots to remove the decaying flesh.

The priest told them that it was the offering of the wine to the gods that blessed the patient, but although Al Farouk agreed with the priest while he was in their presence, he scoffed at the idea that gods had anything to do with the body's recovery among his peers. After all, why would the gods bestow blessings on enemies of Persia? And who were the priests to believe that their divinity ruled above his years of accumulated knowledge? He thought the priests' professional peddlers of vacant and antiquated superstitions, and believed they had conned the aristocracy into financially supporting their empty cause for countless generations under the pretenses of self-proclaimed divinity.

When he was done triaging the soldier's injuries, he had removed an arsenal of spear tips and arrows from the wounded man's body. A few times, the man became pale and clammy during the procedure; the doctor then pumped the soldier's chest until the color returned to his pasty skin. He knew Xerxes wasn't misleading when he told him his fate was tied to the fate of the Spartans, so every effort would be made to keep the men alive.

He railed at his assistants incessantly as they now loaded the broken and bandaged bodies of the soldiers carefully onto plush wagons lined with straw and stacked with soft animal pelts. Skat rolls downhill; the other physicians were now being reminded as Al Farouk redirected his rage at them due to his now dire circumstance. They would not be spared Xerxes' wrath if the Spartan soldiers did not survive their convalescence. He would impose the full scale of Xerxes' rage down on his subordinates, seeming that is what it would take to save his own neck.

After all, the battlefield medics beneath his post imposed this fate upon him in the first place by bringing these wounded men into camp to gain favor rather than just snuffing them on the battlefield. No mistakes or half-measures would be tolerated from now on; it was now incumbent on him to keep the men alive, and there was no other choice.

Dr. Al Farouk and the caravan of wounded soldiers arrived at the jeweled Persian city of Persepolis, deep in the heart of Xerxes' kingdom, as modern a city as any in the world. It was a palatial complex known for the colorful pillars that adorned her many buildings and the many rituals consecrated therein.

In one of the smaller western royal palaces in Persepolis, the prisoners would recuperate in well-guarded confinement to help compound their chances of survival. It was close to the homes of the physicians and other experts in Farouk's field, and there, he had unlimited resources at his disposal.

They were greeted by the head of the palace security, Raza Douul, who escorted the doctors and their patients to this hastily organized, makeshift prison in the bosom of the palace, which was nestled perfectly inside the center ring of the large city; it was also well-staffed with many able-bodied servants. The prisoners were interred in the same wing of the palace where the royal family would be treated for any ailments they might incur when residing there.

Night and day, the doctor tended to the soldiers' wounds personally; he brought and enlisted his best battlefield physicians to care for the gravely wounded men every step of the way. He wrapped the men's wounds with fresh bandages daily and used the Rakki, which they confiscated in the Greek villages and pillaged on the road to Thermopylae. No matter how lofty the effort appeared, these men would not be allowed to perish in their capable hands.

For King Xerxes, it was the fierce gift of survival that he would misleadingly bestow upon the three unlucky Spartans. While the captured men were alive in his captivity, they would be given no honor as soldiers. He had no intention of torturing or abusing these captives to extract military intelligence ... In fact, Xerxes' intentions were quite the opposite, somewhat of a bribe even. The king wanted to understand what primal spirit possessed men such as these. He chose to embarrass them with opulent comforts rather than pain. He just wanted to know why Spartans behaved in battle as they did without fear or regard for personal safety, and how they were bestowed with such a staunch unwillingness to accept defeat.

To him, a man eagerly and proudly embracing a glorious death over survival in a battle was not a typical human; this resolve was the voracity of purpose he longed and thirsted for in his military ranks. Though it genuinely seemed that this trait might not be purchased nor beaten into a man; it could only be forged into his character at a very young age, propagated for a lifetime with careful planning and strict discipline. Xerxes' fear-based leadership did not generate dogged selfless patriotism; loyalty to him was purely a manufactured response beaten into his ranks, much like when a field animal is whipped repeatedly to go in circles pulling a plow. Persian troops performed their function, but not with vigor or the charismatic zeal of these warrior specimens; his men only did what they were required to do, nothing more. They did not rise to the occasion without lashes or a recoiling fear of being forced into harm's way.

Every day, Dr. Al Farouk would lift the most wounded patient's upper torso and lower him back to the table repeatedly, back and forth, pumping the body to get the blood to flow in the places that had been pieced back together. He bent his legs repeatedly to ensure the threads didn't tear out of his skin; he made the medics massage the muscles that were not too severely injured. He assumed that the body was full of blood and that the blood would kill the patient if it settled in one place for too long.

Weeks passed from the day of their discovery; the doctors mainly seemed confident that the wounded men would survive their incredible injuries and live to become the trophies of battle that Xerxes perversely wished for. They still needed constant care and intense rehabilitation to make them mobile again, but this would take time, and who could tell if Xerxes had the patience for all of this? In the meantime, they would be kept sedated and comfortable as much as possible to counter the torment of their rehabilitation and daily stretches.

During one of the first stretching sessions, the most injured soldier awoke from his deep, comatose sleep and opened his eyes. He could not fathom if he was being teased in a palace on Mount Olympus, or was he inside the angry bowels of a necropolis being tortured for his earthly failures? He knew the excruciating pain was a message from Hades. He had heard the elders warn that if you died a coward in battle, you would learn suffering firsthand. The pain was too much, and he faded in and out of his conscious state. Over and over, this moment repeated itself in agony during what seemed like an eternity.

In between these trying moments, he had fever dreams of his mother when he was a small child playing with her in the backyard of their home. He confided to his mother that he had failed his brave king and failed to be the soldier that he was raised to be. For this, he reasoned, he had been thrown into the swirling infernal pit that was now his new home. He told her it had to be Hades ... for where were the rest of his Spartan brothers? Where was his king? They had been whisked off to be with the gods, for he had witnessed their valor and watched some of them drop lifeless in battle after so many devastating charges.

Every day, the torture happened more and more frequently. He would awaken from the breathtaking pain and then pass out cold from it again. He told his mother in the dreams that he deserved this torment because he had fallen in battle. His mother only nodded and wiped the sweat from his brow. She smiled lovingly and stared at him deep in the eyes until he faded and dropped into the dark nothingness.

But there was something strange that he couldn't place. As an infant, he had wrapped his fingers in her dark brown hair as he suckled milk from her breast, but now his mother's hair was almost yellowish white, like fresh-cut straw; but her kindness and gentleness were the same, just as he remembered.

The soldier's name was Panothos … He dreamed every day that this must be Hades, and this must be his punishment for such mediocrity in life, and she must be a guardian spirit sent to witness and potentially validate his suffering.

Day after day, the doctors tended to the men's wounds, and slowly, the Spartan soldiers started healing, slowly recovering and regaining their strength. Xerxes' physicians treated them almost like injured statesmen, offering the healthiest foods, wines, and servant girls to answer

their every need. He needed them to be corruptible,
just like any average man, not invincible by pride
and honor as it was rumored.

At first, the men were puzzled and thought,
why are the Persian captors treating us so well?
Xerxes' method was slowly beginning to win over a
few of the Greek prisoners who were only
tradesmen. They were not trained for the extreme
mental duress of captivity, nor were they willing to
embrace the always impending suffering and
oblivion of a professional warrior in enemy captivity.

But the Spartan soldiers reminded the Greek
men that they might not become endeared to this
place and its posh veiled comforts; it would only be
a temporary station that they must endure with their
honor intact or face dire consequences from within
their ranks. They would never again make the
mistake of dishonoring themselves in battle or life;
they would make certain this time to ensure
themselves a good death.

It took many months for some of the injured
men to regain even the ability to walk unassisted.
The very badly injured and highest rank of the three
Spartans was the warrior Panothos. He had
sustained so many injuries to his torso and
appendages that no other Greek soldiers could
imagine he would ever swing a sword and shield in
battle again. Living by sword and shield was all that
Panothos had ever known since his very short

childhood. He was a student tested, a blade sharpened, bludgeoned, and then forged, then purged and re-sharpened, year after year, time and again.

Even the gods would prefer to skirt around a cohort of these young, rabid, thieving Spartan bastards in training rather than try to progress in a line straight through them. They were like a pack of little rabid hyenas waiting to exploit whichever advantage was left open to them. They suckled blood from their mothers bosom and were born into the gears of a highly efficient and synchronized war machine as legendary as the world would ever know.

Panothos was as strong as men come. He was up and stretching his injured muscles before any of the rest of the severely wounded men did so. As the highest in Spartan rank, his duty was to look after and push his men not to become complacent with the "false" luxuries their cunning and deceitful captors bestowed on them.

On a daily basis, the physicians would come to check on the convalescing Spartan warriors. They would ensure that the recovering soldiers were fed and well-tended, and that there was no chance of them falling ill before Xerxes could do whatever he planned to do with them.

Panothos lay in his cot when Dr. Al Farouk entered with one of the servant girls of the palace.

The doctor stretched Panothos' legs and arms, raising him to his feet. Though drugged, the pain was excruciating, but every day, the same blonde-haired girl would wipe his forehead and massage his muscles as he gasped in pain; she always smelled of lavender and spiced oil.

Concentrating on the girl's exotic scent, he gazed upon her radiant beauty every time the treatments he was given tricked his mind into believing he was about to capitulate and beg mercy from his prodding antagonists. He thought only of screaming out for mercy, and maybe this agonizing pain would end, but he knew that would not be the case, so he welcomed this beautiful distraction every time the doctors put him through these torturous stretches. The doctors, though mildly compassionate, were still enemies of these men and would be persistently cruel in their rehabilitation. They would wash out the healing wounds with spirits and clean them with smooth pumice stone, to the point that Panothos would pass out from the trauma almost every time. Even after all these weeks of convalescence, they still came to experiment, scrape, and pull on him in excruciating ways.

When the doctors became seemingly sadistic, the blonde hair girl became even more gentle and attentive to his suffering. She would knowingly stare into his eyes, noticing that

Panothos would focus on her eyes more when his
suffering increased. Occasionally, when the doctors
were preoccupied with briefing their colleagues, the
girl would gently lean into him and whisper foreign
words into his ear. One word she repeated many
times and emphasized to him was "Gyttja." Though
he didn't know what she was saying, he knew she
was kind and gentle, and imagined it must be her
given name.

Once, she even stepped in front of a doctor
who was being unusually sadistic to Panothos,
objecting to how the doctors were torturing him
instead of helping him. She grabbed one of the
doctor's arms and pulled it away from Panothos just
as it seemed the brutality of the treatment was too
much for him to bear. This insolence was unheard
of amongst the palace servants and was quickly
and unquestionably punishable by death.

But Gyttja was fierce; she unnerved the
educated physician with her exotic blue eyes,
muscular frame, and aggressive reflexive response.
He instantly backhanded her with his other fist, and
she collapsed limp on the floor. This infuriated
Panothos ... but in his condition, he could do nothing
to protect her from the mistreatment. But this
moment gave him a singular purpose, a goal to
focus on ... plotting to someday brutally rain down

cruel vengeance upon these rancid, barbaric captors.

The doctor, an educated and cultured man in his own right, did not see himself as a royal thug. He didn't report the slave's behavior to his superiors or wish to appear as if he were weak, nor did he wish to explain the awkward situation to his peers and fall victim to the psychotic whims of Xerxes, who might want to make an example of him with some insane and diabolical punishment.

He analyzed his situation carefully, and quickly went with his gut feeling that she would not dare do such a thing to him again, especially in front of the glances of others. He would save face with this reflexive, immediate slap and go on about his business as usual with no one any the wiser, forgoing the drama of making the incident widely known.

Panothos could not understand most of what they had said in the altercation. Still, he could feel in his heart that Gyttja was trying to intervene and shield him from further enduring the unimaginable pain inflicted on him. This moment resonated deep in his mind; he would never forget Gyttja's bravery.

Over the course of many treatments, his affection grew for her, as did his understanding of some of her words. She secretly taught him Persian words and some from her dialect; he reciprocated and taught her some words of Greek. They did not yet know it, but their lives and fate would become intertwined like the tangled roots of an olive tree.

The next in rank inside the palace confines was the courageous Aurias. Aurias stood on Panothos' left in the formation of the phalanx. Aurias was a human monster of a man. He stood a head above any of the Persian guards and was chiseled like a statue with long, flowing black hair. As wide as two average men, he bore the brave heart of two. He was the most intimidating of any of the other survivors who were serving out their captivity in the palatial prison.

When the last decapitating charge of the Persian onslaught slammed violently into the Spartan phalanx, a chariot rammed Aurias, fracturing one of his arms, and broke and cracked many of his ribs. He sustained these injuries even after taking multiple arrows through his shoulder and legs. He had been left riddled with contusions, bones protruding from both arms when he was found alive but barely breathing.

Luckily for him, bones heal in time, and scars reinforce the dermis directly at the point of the cut. The wounds grow thicker and more robust than the original skin as the body repairs itself. Aurias had a spectacular temper in war; when ignited, it was a show of violent depravity on a battlefield unlike anyone had seen and lived long enough to speak of.

When the fighting began, a berserk Aurias would see red and go into a crazed battle rage where he would embrace his victims as they fell and look closely into their fading expressions to watch their energy expire. He truly wanted to taste each kill as intimately as possible; it solidified his resolve to survive any battle.

As he approached his next victim in the skirmish, he would look like a possessed demon covered in blood and bits of meat and muscle. He smelled of vomit and wreaked of the insides of a body. Not even beasts in the forest would kill one another with such blatant hostility. He displayed the inhumane byproducts of murder like a grotesque uniform, adorning himself in it entirely for the shock value. It instantly struck primal fear in the hearts of those who would dare raise a sword against him.

Panothos was inspired by Aurias' recovery; every night, he exercised, lifted stones, and helped to raise the Greeks' fighting spirit, methodically remolding the modest stature of the men into the superior standards of a Spartan battle formation.

Though he continuously encouraged the men to rise proudly to this unusual predicament, he rarely spoke of what thoughts lurked deep inside his heart. Aurias knew well that he had unwillingly and unwittingly befallen a dishonor worse than death itself ... and if provoked, he would not hesitate to kill any one of the Greeks if they betrayed his and their one true cause. His singular focus now was only on escaping with his blood brothers.

He instinctively knew he could never return home to Sparta, having been taken captive in battle. He would be deemed a complete failure by the metrics of Spartan society. He would never again be able to see his lover's eyes, nor would he ever again gaze upon his beloved wife, Sericea. Soon, she would learn to dress another man in his armor before battle, wiping away the dust of peace as he readied himself for warfare. He knew he might never learn the outcome of the battle for his homeland, if his efforts were in vain or deemed heroic and worthy of King Leonidas' sacrifice with his many fallen brothers.

Though Sericea would initially cry for his loss, she would soon move on and merely think of him occasionally; even that limited reverence would dissipate over a longer timeline. It was simply the grit of the Spartans; there was no changing this, for these traditions originated in ancient times and served the greater good and perpetuity of the tiny nation-state.

Then, there was the third Spartan warrior recuperating in captivity, Tyranos. This poor, unlucky Spartan soldier had befallen the cruelest life joke of all the survivors ... He sustained a blunt force head injury early in the last day of the battle, trying to push his partner Aurias out of the path of a charging chariot. This injury left him unconscious for a whole changing of the season.

Tyranos was the youngest of the three Spartan survivors. He knew no fear when it came to a battle; he, too, was a man of incredible physique, only a stone's weight smaller than Aurias. When Tyranos was first accepted into the brotherhood of Spartan warriors, he drank too much wine and, on a drunken dare, chased a sacrificial bull that was in rut, billowing in a field behind the barracks, only to come back riding on the rutting bull naked, holding onto it by the horns in a mad dash through the village.

Though the Spartan hierarchy vehemently disapproved of this incoherent display, the cohort to which he was assigned told the story every subsequent year during the Gymnopaedia celebrations; it always brought a roar of laughter and great cheers to the group during the symposium. Not only must you be tough to be a Spartan warrior, but also you must be exceptionally bold. To nakedly expose one's male genitalia to the back of a bucking bull was a feat of bravery even the most calloused warrior would think twice before undertaking, but not Tyranos. He was quick into the fight and fearless in his nature.

He came to in captivity with no significant damage to his body, but something was very different about him when he awoke; he could not think of words at times and would stare blankly into a void like a marble statue obscured in a gilded cage. The doctors had shaved off all of his long, blond, braided mane to drill a hole in his skull and release pressure off the brain; the short hair he now had was unbecoming of a Spartan warrior, making him look much different than Aurias and Panothos.

When Tyranos could finally think somewhat clearly, with Gyttja's help, he snuck into the chamber where Panothos was recuperating. He whispered to his fellow Spartan, "Panothos, my brother, we must find a way out of here! Every day, they steal our souls from us! Something is not right here."

Panothos nodded empathetically. "I know, my friend ... this does not make sense. They do not ask us anything related to our tactics in battle. They are not torturing us for intelligence ... they only try to make us well, it seems; they must be up to something nefarious!"

Gyttja peeked around the corner to ensure the guards did not see the men speaking privately. Tyranos whispered again, "This is not our fate to languish here in captivity, old friend ... I have been given a sign!"

"Tell me what you have seen in your visions, Tyranos."

"Keep an open mind and listen to my dream or vision, whatever it might have been that I witnessed while in one of my blank moments." Continuing, he quietly but firmly whispered, "I thought I must have finally been allowed to feast with the gods on Mount Olympus; small beings surrounded the gods, white-haired angels, or maybe demons ... I could not tell which because they always looked happy and inviting in the eyes but with sardonic, evil smiles on their lips.

"It seemed so crisp and cold there; everything was white with snow ... and children were surrounding me that resembled young soldiers ... and it felt as if I was home ... and that just maybe, they might be 'your' children ..."

Panothos scoffed at Tyranos; knowing all too well the effect of the head injury on his longtime friend, he grimaced and then muttered to himself quietly under his breath ... "Home ... home is now only a memory in the dreams of ghosts."

Tyranos, after attempting to speak once again, began fading out, staring blankly past Panothos' eyes and down into the void of the abyss behind his injured mind. He suddenly rose to his feet and thanked Panothos for his attention, apologizing for focusing on these "otherworldly" matters. Panothos assured him that he was always there for him to speak with, no matter if the subject was otherworldly or not.

Panothos wondered if the warm presence of the girls had given Tyranos these ideas, just as he suspected the visions of his mother were related to the physical trauma and kind nature of the servant girl Gyttja comforting him during his time of need. He walked to the room's opening, and Gyttja motioned for him to follow her back to his chamber.

They were now, for all intents and purposes, ghosts. He and his other Spartan brothers understood this fact deep inside their healing bones; they rationalized that they would never again be able to return home or even speak of home. They already felt as if they were not even worthy in their hearts of calling Sparta their home. Additionally, to make it back to Sparta, they would have to fight through the mighty Persian force that just defeated them, an impossible task.

The remaining warriors were told never to mention their origin again so as not to bring shame down upon their homelands. Aurias made sure they all understood the gravity of the situation; he made the Greeks swear a blood oath on the lives of their former families, never again revealing their true origins. They were cursed to be stateless wanderers from this point forth. This was just how things had to be, and he repeatedly reminded them of it. Though none of the men were pleased with this logic, they understood why it had to be this way and what penalty lay in wait if they chose to stray from this path and welcome Xerxes' tainted offer.

The recovering Spartans took full advantage of their captors' benevolence and ate the healthiest foods they were allowed. All the men quietly befriended the servant girls, who were slaves from far-off lands in the north. These girls spoke a strange language they had never been exposed to before; they had striking eyes as blue as the Aegean, and a gentle nature that warmed the spirits of the men. They wore their blonde hair in long rolled braids; even their eyebrows were white and almost translucent.

Their features were accentuated by their high cheekbones and supple pink lips. The girls looked nothing like the tanned, dark-haired girls of pleasure they knew back in Sparta during their youth. The girls were a welcome distraction from the daily trials the physicians put the men through; they gave them a sense of well-being that these men desperately needed through their brutal rehabilitation.

The Arcadian strategist Kadmos was the oldest and most injured of all the warriors in the palace. He should not have been revived from his battlefield grave. He was now blind, his left hand was amputated in the battle, and he would probably never walk again from the severe damage to both of his legs.

Kadmos had fought hard at the Spartans' side; he was severely injured on the first day of the battle but chose to stay and keep fighting the onslaught. His fellow Arcadians also stayed and rallied with him, keeping in step with his incredible bravery. Kadmos understood the tactics of the incoming invaders, and his unit effectively pivoted to repel them every time they tried to outflank them. He managed to keep many of his soldiers alive until the final overwhelming volley on the last day of their resistance. Even bedridden, he would get messages to Panothos via Gyttja, pointing out weak spots in the palace defenses and ideas of how to escape.

The prisoners trained their bodies to acclimate to and accept pain; it was an always-present reminder that they must flee this captive existence. They would try to push through this impasse with an unrelenting focus as a group. Kadmos always imparted in them a desire to escape and somehow evade capture while still ultimately avenging the honor of their fallen brothers who had perished that day at the Battle of Thermopylae. They knew they would never see their homelands again but could not play this insane waiting game much longer; they had to find a way out soon. As far as Kadmos was concerned, this was the only way to vindicate themselves in the eyes of the fallen and reach Olympus.

During the daylight hours in captivity, while the highest-ranking officers were present in the palace, the interred men acted as if their wills had been broken and they were now just hobbling feeble wretches; lazy, forgotten prisoners languishing inside a cell. They shuffled and dragged their feet when walking, and always looked down at the ground and away from the eyes of the overseeing guards. However, they still occasionally took beatings from Raza Douul, depending on how foul his mood was on a particular day.

The pattern of the men's routine became sleeping late, complaining to the doctors about their pain, and acting unwell during the daylight hours. When the lights were out, they were quietly exercising and planning what their next moves would be going forward ... Though their honor was tarnished, typically, you cannot erase a man's dignity so easily, especially with men like these who were molded from tempered sheets of hardened iron. From the armor of Zeus, they were conceived and clad, and all the way to Olympus, they would climb to be free of this enduring spectacle, paraded around as living trophies for a delusional barbarian king.

With the aid of a walking stick, Panothos was finally able to move around in the great vault in which they were interred. One evening, he snuck into Kadmos' chambers to plot their escape with him.

"You should have stayed in your bed, Panothos," he was told by Kadmos.

Panothos replied, "We need to speak, my friend. I know the way from here, but to where I am uncertain."

"You will know your direction when it becomes necessary, Panothos," Kadmos quipped.

"But I do not know how we will move you from here, dear friend. You are not at all in the right condition to be moved, and I know you are aware of this. Nor do I believe, old friend, that you will ever be mobile again, and it truly pains me."

"I know, and I am under no delusions at all. You 'will' leave me here and save your and my men's skins!" Kadmos growled under his breath. "I know my time here is short. This is no life. I am a warrior like you; I am very aware that my future's breaths are numbered."

"I cannot believe we must say these things, Kadmos, we must ..."

"Wait!" Kadmos replied. "You must stop thinking of me in your plans; I am no longer viable.

Now is not the time for weakness; you must strike and strike hard when the right time comes. There is no future here for any of us; you of all know this. This opulence is only a tactic to distract us from our purpose—survival, and freedom. Neither will exist without the other.

"I need you to take my remaining men somewhere they may start over! I know your Spartan honor wants you to be overthrown in battle. But why, Panothos? These men have given their whole life to this cause. By my understanding of our injuries, we should all be dead, but we are not. This gives us notice that this subtle captivity is only a ploy to render our stand useless in the eyes of history, creating a subservient world where others will not rise up and stand against the advances of these ruthless tyrants!

"We must not let this come to pass! And I will not seek comfort here, even in my wretched condition, no matter the pain it causes me. This is where we differentiate ourselves from the barbarians; this is where history will know our names as carriers of the light."

Panothos bowed his head; he knew Kadmos spoke only in truths.

"The girls are your salvation, Panothos. Have you learned this yet?" His voice now quivered from duress. "You must put aside your old ideas and adapt to this moment. Forget your old life and befriend these girls; they are your only true weapon inside this place!"

Panothos sat quietly, digesting Kadmos' words. It winded Kadmos not only because of his present condition but also because of his genuine belief that his men deserved a second chance after seeing their unwavering bravery on the battlefield. They had died once, and there was no need to suffer the same fate twice. Panothos, a humbled man, thanked Kadmos and snuck back to his own chambers to contemplate his next steps.

Another season passed, and the small group of men, Greeks and Spartans, lived well-disciplined lives, studying the battle strategy and learning to become professional soldiers again. From generations of Spartan warrior tradition, the Greeks absorbed the principles of Spartan military tactics and battle formations. In turn, the Spartans learned the basic tenets of carpentry and mathematics from the Greek tradesmen. Panothos knew they would all need these skills if they were to stand any chance outside the city's walls; to survive and evade capture was only the first part of the plan, but long-term survival in a foreign land would be contingent on obtaining a variety of valuable skill sets.

Xerxes remained away from the city for a long time; his guard was very tight-lipped about his movements, even amongst its ranks; none in the palace knew of his whereabouts until a few hours before his arrival. In despotic kingdoms such as this, tyrants always become paranoid of assassination attempts, obsessing over every detail until they compromise their own freedom and sanity. Though palace gossip ran rampant among the servants and staff, these privileged pieces of intelligence were rare and unusual.

The men hoped there would be more time and warning before Xerxes returned and revealed his real intentions. They knew this lavish captivity didn't make any sense and would eventually evolve into some new kind of torment to endure. They understood that Xerxes' intentions could not be any good for them.

After many months, the soldiers' premeditated patterns and patience began paying off. Learning to communicate with some of the servant girls gave the men the lay of the land and a decent understanding of the world outside of the palace's walls. The girls described potential weak spots in the security on the perimeter of Persepolis' royal quarter and the sewer tunnels, which led to a dry creek outside the walls. The girls also told stories of their homelands, a cold destination in a faraway land where they could escape if they could find the will and the fortitude to make such an arduous journey …

They explained that it was a harsh land where everything must be earned, but the fishing was good, and the people were tough and uncompromising. It was a place where the sunlight on summer days seemed never to end, and the winter nights were so long you would believe the sun might never rise again.

It all sounded like some strange fairy tale to the Spartans, but they were truly intrigued; such unknown lands would offer them the almost certain anonymity they desired and a possible future. But as with anything, there was a caveat; the beautiful blonde servant girls wanted desperately to return to this place and do so with the help of these brave warriors. The girls could envision their exit clearly for the first time since they were cast into this forced servitude so long ago.

The ladies constantly flirted with the men, told the men story after story of good hunting, and spoke of an intoxicating drink they called "mead," which they made from yeast and honey. They had been away from home for so many years that they feared their families would have forgotten their faces or must surely think them dead by now.

Panothos thought very highly of the girls … especially Gyttja. They were the perfect allies; they were tough, intelligent, and extremely beautiful, and after so many docile years in captivity, they were trusted by the palace guards. This was a hidden advantage that the men would exploit to gain the upper hand in their situation, to blur their captors' focus. The Persian officers viewed the females as weak and subservient, so the girls had unencumbered freedom of movement inside and outside the palace walls, here so deep inside the Persian borders.

They were tasked daily with retrieving supplies from the market and cooking for and serving all of the palace's inhabitants. They served the officers and guards first, then the captives, maintaining the day-to-day chores of the palace grounds. Panothos surmised that the girls had a fundamental knowledge of the surroundings and a burning desire to be free again, and they knew of an actual destination where they could go to escape and live free from this captivity, hopefully for the rest of their days.

Panothos began incorporating the ladies into his escape plans. The combination of brains and the overwhelming power of female seduction, which would virtually neutralize most of the guards, made the girls a covert weapon in the Spartan arsenal. But only the light-skinned, blue-eyed girls had the fire in their hearts to leave the palace and conspire with the recovering men. Many of the other girls were contented to live a "good life" here in their plush captivity, better than the life they had back in their homelands.

Panothos learned from Gyttja that some of the poor girls' families had even sold them into this vile servitude to gain wealth and status. This amazed and repulsed him; *How perverse*, he thought, *the cruel fathers, who would sell away their daughters so easily and for mere table scraps of wealth or influence*. Panothos imagined that it would be good to have the company of these pale and beautiful new partners on whatever course fate and this life had chosen for them. At best, they could start over together. At worst, they were strong women unafraid to defend themselves or do what needed to be done to escape and persevere!

Chapter 2

Small Steps

The capital city of Persepolis ... A sprawling metropolis deep in the guarded heart of Persia, one of the golden cities of the ancient world. Inside this ceremonial centerpiece of the crown, fear of the barbarian king's tyrannical rule kept its citizenry firmly in check simply by the threat of violence and retribution. When asked their opinion about their leader, the local population always cheered, "Long live Xerxes!" But the words fooled no one; anybody could tell it was only a reflex statement, not an honest, heartfelt gesture. It was just expected of them, and they said it to alleviate any unnecessary suffering that might be inflicted on them or their families by the royal Susian Guard.

The guard, which the Immortals commanded, brutally enforced the edicts of King Xerxes and demanded unwavering patriotism with an extremely heavy hand. They had a sinister reputation for forcing Xerxes' will on subjects, and no one was truly safe, no matter the social status or fealty shown to the king; they all feared brutal and severe reprisal for any action the guard perceived to be against the regime.

Gyttja approached Panothos one afternoon in the bathhouse as Panothos steamed his aching body. Gyttja pulled a cloth towel from a ledge and walked over to Panothos to wrap him in it and massage his neck and back. The guards had become complacent with their movements and walked out of the room to sit and rest their feet and gamble with the other sentries.

Gyttja leaned close into Panothos' shoulder and whispered into his ear, "Panothos, I need to tell you something; I overheard the officers speaking during their dinner last night. Xerxes plans to return after the upcoming holy day, but they did not say which day exactly. They said he was coming back to check on his 'pets.'" Panothos instantly tensed up.

He turned his head to the side to look out for the guards; he looked at Gyttja out of the corner of his eyes, she appeared very concerned with the news she had delivered.

"I believe you are a powerful man who has done incredible things and can accomplish many more. I believe fate has put you in my life, in our lives, for a reason. I don't yet know this reason, but I have an idea what it might be. I believe I dreamed of this moment when I was a little girl, but I didn't understand what the dream was about, and now I need to do what I feel deep in my heart because the dream is beginning to make sense to me now!

"When do you plan to leave this place, Panothos, and will you take us when you do? Please?" she asked, almost desperately. "I wish to see my homeland again, away from this place and this servitude, as do the others. I yearn to smell the pine forest of my childhood!"

Panothos quietly nodded yes to her; Gyttja smiled, immediately latching her arms around Panothos, holding him tightly. All the stress melted away from his aching body; even the pain was now silent as she embraced him. After a few moments, his sense of duty overcame his emotions, and he flexed his shoulders. She released her embrace in case the guard looked in upon them. But before she let go, he felt her bosom pressed tightly against his body, arousing his senses; it was a feeling he had missed but hadn't realized quite how greatly during his captivity.

Gyttja's beauty was a welcome distraction during this time of great suffering. It had been so long since he had honestly felt he could enjoy anything. But now, the warmth of her body and her tight embrace struck a nerve and brought his blood back to its correct temperature, setting off carnal feelings he had not felt in so very long; it made him feel young!

Looking her in the eyes, he said, "But please tell me this: what will give us an upper hand that none of these guards could expect or foresee,

Gyttja? We need something other than violence alone; we don't have the right weapons for a full assault on the guard posts. We must escape quietly, stealthily from the city, or we will have no chance of survival."

She sighed, contemplating his modest lament for a moment, and then answered, "Outside the walls of this palace, there is one thing that these people do ... a thing I have never seen anywhere in my days as a young girl ... Many of the local people here cover their faces with scarves; maybe due to the dry climate and dust, and some most likely from their local customs or religion."

He gazed at her lips when she spoke, which she noticed but didn't let on. Her cheeks instantly flushed with color, which he noticed but didn't acknowledge due to the seriousness of their conversation. He nodded and thanked her for the information.

"This knowledge is so valuable to us, Gyttja; I will tell you the path we choose to embark on, but know this one thing is for certain: I will be taking you and the other girls with me; you may count on this!"

A relaxed mood washed over her; there was finally a real possibility of leaving this place.

Thinking this information was an incredibly valuable piece of actionable intelligence, Panothos finally fully envisioned his direction. It needed to be as simple of a plan as possible to be realistic in its scope and achievability. He quickly finished dressing and quietly made his way to Kadmos and the other two Spartans to explain his idea.

He moved as quickly as he had in many months, invigorated by the prospect of an exodus from this palatial prison. Panothos would use this new information so they might try and gain a tactical advantage over their Persian captors and escape the palace peacefully with their heads still attached to their bodies before Xerxes spoiled any well-tailored plans with an unannounced return. He knocked softly and entered Kadmos' room. He motioned for Panothos to approach. Aurias and Tyranos soon followed him into the room.

Panothos quietly relayed what Gyttja had told them; Aurias clenched his fists in untethered anticipation. They thought this almost too good to be true, an unquestioned cloak to walk freely in public without drawing attention to themselves. Aurias asked, "Is she trying to set us up to gain some power in the palace hierarchy? This seems too simple."

Kadmos shook his head, raised his hand, and quieted him. Panothos interjected, "No, I know she has no ill intentions; she is enslaved with us and has been here for years. She is a woman of strong character; she stood up for me when I was too weak to defend myself and has truly earned my

52

trust and full gratitude. She yearns for her freedom, as do we."

Aurias proposed, "If we could clandestinely make it outside of the fortified walls of this disgusting prison, we could cover our faces with this headdress and blend seamlessly into the population, but that is only if we can find a silent way out of the palace without raising any alarms or engaging in an open conflict with the stationed guards."

It seemed plausible, but they understood that time was woefully against them, and they needed to escape as soon as possible. They knew avoiding the myriad unforeseen possibilities of imposed change was paramount to their survival. The possibility of Xerxes returning, relocating, or separating the group was becoming more and more of a frightening reality. If it happened, they would again be at Xerxes' mercy, completely without allies or an upper hand. Panothos reasoned with his comrades, "The time to put our plan into action is now, but we need to find some cover to camouflage our insurrection." Aurias agreed and then retreated to his quarters.

Now firmly on the road to recovery, they thought of nothing but escape. Regardless of impending hazards and obstacles, they had plotted relentlessly just for this day, the day of their emancipation. Even to die escaping would be an act of Spartan courage, and still better than the polished purgatory in which they were currently being forced to exist.

After many months of watching the convalescing captives limp around the palace, the guards had grown quiet and complacent. The boredom of the day-to-day rehabilitation of the captives and the calm politeness of the ailing men had left their senses languid and their resolve deflated.

Panothos accumulated some basic Persian phrases from Gyttja and used them as often as possible. The prisoners could now partially communicate with the guards, which also lulled the guards into bad habits and lax surveillance. Believing that the beleaguered Spartans were genuinely beginning to assimilate peacefully into their new existence, some younger guards almost began to regard the Greeks as foreign guests. Panothos knew that once outside the walls, a few simple words of the language would also be a helpful way out of some potentially bad situations. In all his studies as a young man, the one thing that had always held true for all situations was that knowledge is power, and battles are usually won or lost in the mind.

Over these months that Panothos was in the torturous care of the Persian physicians, he and all the men had been given a strange bitter medicine that made you forget about all your pain; it made your every care evaporate into a soft pillow of endless waking dreams. The doctors would lacerate and milk the bulb of a high desert plant, the poppy, and convert its nectar into an orally ingested elixir; the pain would almost seem to vanish into thin air with this substance.

But the soldiers were tough men who could manage the pain without the help of the elixir. Hence, they began secretly storing the medicine in small sheep bladders that one of the girls had smuggled in from outside the palace walls. Gyttja made her rounds collecting the oil from the different patients whenever she was given access to their chambers.

Though the pain was nearly unbearable, Panothos and the other wounded men endured it with relaxed faces and stone-like demeanors, faking the potion's effects after it was supposedly administered. Although they regained their physical strength, they acted as if the pain was unbearable whenever the doctors checked on them and performed their stretches. Thinking it a great way to keep the men docile, the physicians kept them at very high doses. Throughout the time spent in their rehabilitation, they managed to collect a decent amount of this bitter and very precious nectar for later use, seeing its potential as a silent weapon early on in their captivity.

Time passed quickly, and it was time for the annual Persian festival of Khordad Sal, which Gyttja warned them of. It was the only time of the year that the guards would be preoccupied with ancient rituals and over-the-top displays of goodwill towards one another. Panothos wagered that the cheerful attitude should most likely weaken the soldiers' resolve on duty.

The higher-ranking guards were at home drinking and celebrating with their families just as the girls informed them; the newer subordinate guards were left overseeing the prisoners in confinement. In the palace guard hierarchy, the newer guards were just one level above the slaves; they were yelled at like servants and were made to oversee any unpleasant work inside the palace walls by the slaves. Panothos quickly realized that these men's weak resolve would be a fault to be exploited upon the day of their exit.

Finally, the time of offerings arrived; the people fasted and prayed for three days. They celebrated the birth of Zarathustra on the final day, and in the night, lavish feasts welcome the end of fasting. The streets were filled with vendors, pilgrims, and priests. A spicy smoke billowed from the many pits that filled the street, and the smell of cooking lamb and goat wafted past the masses of colorful, wondrously adorned processions who snaked around the city chanting in now long-forgotten tongues. Dust rose high into the night from these processions that joined the many caravans of pilgrims and worshipers. A marvelously festive mood engulfed the whole city, quickly infecting anyone participating in the celebrations.

The palace servant girls adorned themselves with perfumes and the most beautiful outfits they had at their disposal, purposely exposing the cleavage of their bosoms and making them visually accessible to the younger, naive guards' prying eyes. They giggled and flirted with the young men, which the recruits were unfamiliar with.

The young guards became completely enamored by the girls and openly welcomed their seductive advances. These men were never allowed to entertain the slave girls in front of their commanding officers; they were told they were part of the king's haram, which made them even more exotic and out of reach to the guards.

So now, on this wildly festive evening, they happily welcomed the girl's playful advances and enjoyed this forbidden time away from the watchful eyes of their commanders. Being the object of the women's affections was all that most of them secretly wished for at night in their bunks. Most of the soldiers were still virgins due to the highly conservative military guild in which they were yoked in service.

All the while, the commanders were away feasting and celebrating, leaving the young recruits to their own devices. Once the sun went down, the girls fed them dried fruits, flatbreads, olives, and cheeses; they kept pushing the salted foods down the desirous guards' throats.

Much earlier in the day, just after the morning prayers, on this final day of celebration, the girls at the direction of Panothos divided up the saved opium elixir and spiked it inside a fruit drink mixed with Aragh Sagi, a Persian moonshine, which the girls had prepared weeks before, for the culmination of the night's feast. Once the delicious salty food had been delivered to all the posts and devoured, the girls brought the thick, sweet drink to the overnight guards stuck on duty during the festivities. For the guards, after so many days of fasting, after all the salty treats, the effect worked better than could have been imagined ...

To ensure the guards consumed enough of the drink for it to work effectively, Gyttja made the dose as heavy as possible but still not so much as to be detectable by taste. They experimented on the local Arabic slave girls before they gave the drinks to the guards; the Arab girls were not included in their plan and were seen as potential antagonists who might expose them for an elevation of status in the palace hierarchy, so to measure the amount they could get away with, they were used as guinea pigs to find the proper dosage and remove them as another unknown variable inside the palace walls they might have to contend with on this night. In this case, a fatal dose to the guards or other slaves was considered entirely acceptable. They would have poisoned the whole lot if they'd had enough of the substance. Still, the limited supply had to be measured to optimize the desired effect.

The majority of the Arab girls and guards finally entered into the hypnotic slumber from the tainted drink, drifting into a deep and comforting stupor. The girls hastily checked all the corners of the palace to verify that all the guards and Arab girls were incapacitated. They all slumped with perverse smiles, and saliva dripped from the corners of their mouths.

After this, Panothos and the Greeks made easy, calm work of their escape. They suggestively posed the guards and the Arab slave girls naked where they lay, so that when their superiors found them, they would initially be blamed for sexual fraternization and gross insubordination.

As the guards nodded and drifted in and out of unconscious dreams, Panothos and the other Greeks made their move. A few guards were large boys who didn't go down as quickly from the drink ... Aurias crept silently up behind their positions with a stolen blade. The guards were squinting and confused, eyes rolling back in their heads, staggering and trying to find their balance through the chemical haze that had descended rapidly upon them. He slit their throats silently; one tried to scream, but when the dagger sliced into his neck, it ended in a gurgling noise of air escaping through the hole in his throat as he quietly asphyxiated on his own blood. Aurias left them to quietly bleed out face down in the warm running water in the servant baths.

Now that all resistance inside the palace had been gracefully quelled, the men had only a few desperate hours to make a great distance between themselves and the city, far away from here, before the doctors and day commanders would check in and find the outpost evacuated and devastatingly lethargic.

Panothos quickly entered Kadmos' room to see to him before they left, and his Arcadian brothers surrounded him. "How are you doing, my friend?"

"My heart is joyful; I am delighted to see you all off this glorious day!" Kadmos replied with glee.

Panothos wanted to protest about leaving him here alone, but Kadmos spoke again before a word could escape Panothos' lips. "My dear friends, it is time for you to leave, to live. Please look at me in my current state and understand that this is no way for me to exist. I am not a young man; I have lived two of many of your lives. I have loved many women, fought powerful enemies greater than myself, and have been victorious. I should not have been revived this time. It is not of nature, and I do not want to go on this way; please understand me." The room sulked.

"Lovely Gyttja has left me a delicious drink that I will enjoy as the morning guards find what you have done. I will relish the chaos of their undoing. You will find your way to a better life, and please think of me laughing at their befuddlement as you make your way to freedom. Now, please, be gone with you; I would like to rest."

The men did as he requested, heading down into the kitchen. Panothos looked back at Kadmos, who sipped a taste of the delicious fruity drink and smiled.

The group exited from the palace through the waste tunnels under the floors, access to which Gyttja made sure remained unlocked so the celebratory mess could be cleaned before the commanding officers arrived the following morning. The tunnels snaked underground past a stable and split in four directions, enabling their egress near the creek.

This was the golden evening of their liberation, the night where they again became free men by their own will and by their own capable hands; the night that they had contemplated for multiple seasons was now upon them, and they would sooner die fighting rather than live on their knees beholden to an illegitimate, ignominious tyrant!

The escapees wrapped themselves in scarves the servant girl Sigrun smuggled in to not draw extra attention to themselves. They now quietly exited the palace through shafts that led down into the sewer tunnels under Persepolis rather than through a main entrance where they might be easily discovered.

It was a filthy place full of disgusting smells and scurrying rodents. Luckily, the scarves they wrapped around their faces had been stored in the same chest as the girl's lavender oils, which helped to hold back the nauseating smells as they wormed through these littered, ancient sewers.

They snaked back and forth through the maze of the vastly overburdened tunnel system. It was all they could do not to collapse from the noxious odor. They finally surfaced out of the drains inside the stalls of the public stables near the creek. They avoided stealing horses this close to the city center to avoid drawing unnecessary attention.

Exiting the stables carefully, they integrated their group into the crowded streets in pairs. They wormed their way around guard posts, consumed by the crowd noise and the boisterous atmosphere bursting freely around them. They followed in and carefully merged their ranks into the processions, dancing and chanting around the city center. The sound of chanting, animal skin drums, and cheers reverberated in swirling circles around the lively city.

The Pulvar River was at its lowest level during the celebration; during this, the driest period of the year, it didn't back up into the creek and wash up into the sewer system until the monsoons arrived later in the season. Luckily so, otherwise the prisoners would have had to fight their way out of the main palace entrance, earning every step of their escape with only rudimentary, quickly fashioned weapons and enough gall to try and win the day with force.

Most of the Greeks were well enough rested, mostly healed, and ready to escape. They seemed as if they were strong enough and organized enough to move quickly and quietly. Only a few men had to be helped along in the tunnels due to their prior, still-healing injuries. Panothos traveled shockingly well for the hideous state he had been in just a few seasons earlier. He had to carry a staff to aid in his movement, which made him seem older, but it also served as a weapon for when he might need to defend himself.

After a half hour, they finally came to the edge of one of the outer neighborhoods closest to the river's edge and began to separate from the endless masses of pilgrims. They formed two groups and hugged the shadows of the river's path. Many of the guards in the city had given in to the joviality of the festival. They feasted with the pilgrims who surrounded their posts, sharing their food and homemade fermented drinks.

Led by Gyttja and the servant girls, each group would follow the winding riverbank behind the now-shuttered bazaar and make their way to the north. This was the plan, at least, but they all knew that plans could easily go awry quickly and unravel without warning.

When the last groups finally crept past the guards' view, they merged back together as one entity. They borrowed some flatboats moored on the riverbank the pilgrims had traveled into the city with. They pushed hard upstream, rowing through the remaining hours of darkness with all the strength they could summon. Free ... but in a foreign and hostile land, with the pending callous sun about to rise at their back and expose their silent exit. They rowed through the current forcefully, trying to get as far away from the city as possible.

At least for now, there was some distant chance for a dignified existence rather than one of unbefitting dishonor and perpetual enslavement. This attempt could reinstate some of the pride the men had honed since they were small boys in Mother Greece. The servant girls stared upstream daringly into the future, now with some prospects for a simple but good life anchored deeply in each of their hearts.

Each person in the group was painfully aware in their own silent thoughts of the price this hard-earned freedom may cost and the trials they must surely face to see their honor restored. Salvation would not be cheap; it would test them to the brink of what they could each endure.

Panothos stared at Gyttja as she dug into the water with an oar, her glances visible in the sallow moonlight. She was tough and fearless to have been willing to set out on this risky undertaking with this group of injured prisoners. She and the other servants were women of honor and courage, brave maidens who did not fear sword nor shield. He could not have asked for better people to conspire with. Panothos would try with all his strength to keep them safe; he also felt they would reciprocate this act for him.

Later, in the early morning's still darkness, the sun's light began to tint the darkened eastern sky with whispers of color, and began to paint a delicate line on the base of the horizon in softened hues. Water lapped gently and rhythmically at the boats' sides as they cut their way upstream.

Panothos told the group to halt and stood at the back of the leading vessel with his eyes focused on their rear; he could make out the very faint but almost regal tone ... The faint sound reverberated off the valley walls' rock face, catching Panothos' ear. The noise was the official confirmation that the narrow breach they exploited overnight had been discovered.

The palace horns of Persepolis were wailing away, far downstream in the distance. They had put a fair distance between themselves and the enemy forces. Still, the upper hand was now fading like the cloak of darkness in the night sky, exposing the grim realities that were being broadly heaped before them. The men knew that the next step was crucial: finding enough horses to move at the same rate or faster than the Persian cavalry, which would undoubtedly soon be locked fervently on their trail.

Chapter 3

Divine Providence

Commander Samid Al Sahan, the most ruthless of Xerxes' Susian officer corps, was an ogre of a man, not in stature but in his natural raw temperament. He was ravenous for power, focusing on acquiring as much of it as could be grasped by his greedy, blood-stained hands.

He was the man who falsely boasted to Xerxes that his maneuver in Southern Greece at the Anopaia path ultimately brought the Western swine to their bent and bleeding knees. However, he was unaware that the bulk of the Greek army had escaped in the night and lived to fight another day.

He desired to be the Persian officer corps' most decorated and celebrated commander. He went so far as to publicly state to his underlings that he would gladly kill his sons for insubordination in battle if they were so weak as to deface themselves and his good name as cowards. Captain Samid was an overly proud man capable of unthinkable atrocities on and off the battlefield.

His uniform was ornate, trimmed in gold chains; his swords, which he always carried two of, were sheathed inside jeweled scabbards and decorated with the teeth of his conquered foes, deeply embedded in the wood amongst the precious stones.

He was a boastful rogue who would purposely leave his men to die on the battlefield if he felt their spirit was too weak for his masochistic tastes. Samid was notorious for killing his wounded officers because he exclaimed, "If you chose to fight like cowards and let yourself become wounded, you didn't fulfill your obligation to me, Persia, your men, or the king!"

Samid would continue to explain, "To me, you are as useless as a parasite, consuming the resources that should be reserved only for real soldiers." He would offer to end a wounded man's suffering only if the man apologized for his failure as a warrior; he would then instruct his guards to decapitate the man to save face for his family so they would still be compensated for his service to the kingdom.

He surmised that a man's family should not be held financially responsible for their husband and father's lack of heart in the field. This was not a common practice among Xerxes' commanders. Still, Xerxes welcomed the cruelty and brutal effectiveness of how Samid operated. He expected nothing less than total and complete allegiance to the regime!

Samid awoke to the sound of horns loudly trumpeting in west Persepolis; something was amiss. He was the first to rise to the brash alarm. He rushed to the source of the palace horns; as he approached, he realized the worst of all the things he could imagine happening had come to bear: Xerxes' unusual prize had escaped into the night.

He viewed this turn of events somewhat perversely, as if the gods had thrust a gift of divine providence directly into his waiting hands. He knew that if his forces were to recover the escaped prisoners, he would be promoted to one of the highest positions in the empire, reigning with more power than even the head of the clergy.

Circling and scolding his men as they mounted up for the chase ... he boasted that if they could not retrieve a small, insignificant group of wounded medical patients to face the king's wrath, then they had no reason to remain in this world breathing the same air as he.

The reward he offered his men for the prisoners' capture? To remain alive ... to simply not be executed ... failure was not an option to even be considered by his men, and any failure whatsoever would end in either one's suicide or execution. For this reason, Samid's soldiers were thrust into their own fight for survival, and they would not relent until Panothos and the others were made to bow in disgrace before their supreme commander and beg for their lives.

Before marching out, Samid dismounted his horse. He stomped into the palace, where Raza Douul and Dr. Al Farouk stood in disbelief. They had also answered the morning alarm. Without saying a single word, Samid unleashed his fury on the doctor. He pulled both swords from his scabbards, crossed his blades, and pulled down sweepingly, instantly severing Farouk's head from his body; Raza Douul gasped.

It happened so quickly that Al Farouk witnessed his torso hitting the cold floor before his brain stopped processing the spectacle. His last thought, clearly in an acute state of shock, was how incredible the human brain must be in its infinite design to have a few more seconds of contemplation left, even as it is separated from its host and rolling on the floor. Samid angrily kicked the head across the room as he exited the palace, leaving a bloody streak on the once-white marble tiles.

Samid scowled at Raza Douul and yelled, "Well, do you plan to try and fix this mess or just stand there looking like a complete fool?"

The Persian soldiers grouped as fast as they could into battle columns, dust rising from their ominous ranks, gossiping about what had just happened inside the palace with the doctor's now-decapitated body. The men were shocked but invigorated with a unique sense of hatred for these devious prisoners. After witnessing what had just transpired in the palace with the doctor, they knew that not a single man in their ranks was safe. They were enraged that their colleagues allowed the prisoners to escape in the first place. But now, these pompous Greeks had inadvertently put their lives in danger, even after Persia had shown them such incredible kindness in captivity.

They viciously whipped their steeds and rode out of the palace in a full lathered gallop, 120 men strong. Focusing on nothing but capturing and killing these ungrateful fugitives, they dug in their heels and thrust themselves into the manhunt. A plume of choking dust followed them like a specter; the ground shook like the gods themselves were protesting in an angry cadence that cut heavily across the dry land.

As far as Samid was concerned, everything in their path would be scrutinized and decimated without prejudice if he saw fit. If the villagers on the outskirts of Persepolis hadn't tried to stop the prisoners themselves, they would be guilty of collusion, and they, too, would be put to death by his swords. This was the rule in Persia: tyrant middlemen who would snuff out life as quickly as they would extinguish a candle or crush a trespassing ant under a hoof. There was no heart beating with mercy in this cruel man's overly decorated chest, only a dogged will for power and an unquenchable thirst for human trophies. He loved this sport and revered it as glorious; warfare, wealth, and power were unapologetically precisely what he desired.

Panothos, an honorable and decent man, was well aware that the Persian commanders were this calculatedly cruel; he had witnessed their wicked brutality personally. He bet his life and the lives of all with him on how he imagined the Persian forces would react to their cunning deception and give chase. His plan was simple: to use the enemy's rage as a constant antagonizing force, to keep them agitated and off-balance as they advanced, to make them sacrifice themselves to their fears and emotions. He thought it better to die fighting this callous enemy than languishing in a prison cell like a caged tiger on display in a human circus.

Panothos and his men saw faint smoke from some settlement far ahead as they pushed forward. They landed the boats and continued on foot. Panothos sent scouts ahead to find out what was making the smoke. The scouts quickly returned, informing him that it looked like a medium-sized encampment, maybe eighty or so soldiers in temporary shelters garrisoned in a small perimeter, with a cluster of large canvas military tents primarily in the center. Panothos assumed that these soldiers, too, had been celebrating in the great feast throughout the night. They may also be easily caught off-balance, presumably still asleep in their tents where they deemed themselves safely distant from any credible military threat.

The Greeks were highly outnumbered, but from the description of the scout's reconnaissance, these men were just a reserve or maybe part a training facility. Primarily boys and old men, by the looks of it, only a few posted sentries at best; Panothos reasoned they were deep inside their own lands, so strategically, the need for higher security was nominal.

He sent the two scouts forward again to the high ground in front of the entrance to the small outpost. When Panothos approached the position, creeping silently out of the shadows, the men pointed out exactly where the weak spots were located and where they saw the camp's strengths. They advised him on which entrance to attack first, to better capitalize on their confusion and inflict the quickest damage.

The Persian army was known to steal children. They made orphans when they conquered a land; they would conscript the boys into such units. The outpost was probably half populated with scared little boys taken from their dead families or sequestered lands under Persian occupation.

Those children yearned for home and family but were thrust into a violent life of military training and endless servitude.

The sun began to peak from the horizon, warming the morning air. At this hour, the oldest students and commanders were rousing from their tents for the early morning prayer when devastation began to reign down from high. Aurias and the Greeks ferociously attacked in a violent human tempest. From three sides of the camp, rocks started dropping like small missiles, knocking some of the soldiers unconscious, caving in and collapsing their skulls and faces, crumpling them into lifeless heaps exactly where they stood. They had been stretching seconds earlier, and now their light was being extinguished by the fierce blows.

Aurias had made slings from anything he could get his hands on during their escape from Persepolis: bandages, linens from the palace, and bits of rawhide they happened across in the stables. The weapons seemed crudely fashioned, but their effectiveness was acute. He had the scouts stack medium-sized river stones in small ammunition dumps at a few positions they believed best to launch the improvised attack from. They pressed hard and fast to get inside the camp as quickly as possible, keeping the young trainees on their heels from the onset of contact. Once in, Panothos let the well-trained men do what they had prepared rigorously for ... close-up, organized, unapologetic, synchronized killing.

Once inside the camp's perimeter, Tyranos and the Greeks bent down, grabbing the wounded students' swords and spears scattered about the compound's grounds underneath the slumped bodies that had buckled from the first volley of stone projectiles. In Tyranos' capable hand, the sword was like an organic appendage. He wielded it with a precision that frightened the poorly resisting Persians. They fled the assault so rapidly that Tyranos had to run behind them and give chase.

He rounded a tent, and finally, the officers in charge and some of the older students rallied and formed a small defensive formation. This put a smile on Tyranos' face; he looked at his Greek counterpart Demetrios, who had a serious look of consternation molded to his. Tyranos nodded and asked Demetrios, "Are you ready, my friend?"

Demetrios nervously nodded, and Tyranos charged the line with the Hoplite by his side. Demetrios thought, *The Spartans are either the bravest men I've ever witnessed or the craziest* ... either way, he was happy to be fighting on the same side as he charged with them!

The first Persian officer lunged forward with a quick thrust of his sword, but Tyranos pivoted and countered as their blades met with a resounding crash. The attack left the Persian soldier off-balance, and Tyranos swiped at his leg, leaving a gash the length of his thigh; then, with a sudden jolt, Tyranos turned entirely in a circle and landed a devastating blow on the soldier's collarbone, sinking the blade deep into his chest, sending the Persian officer crashing down to the ground.

As the man collapsed, the others scurried away from the skirmish, fearing the same fate. The remaining students and officers who had been trying to repel the assault all retreated, terrified and screaming, running from the bloody scene of Tyranos' butchery, and leaving their ranks tattered and in absolute disarray. Tyranos looked around and could find no more resistance to butcher.

Then, the sound every soldier waits to hear on the battlefield, the strange misplaced silence of the other side's capitulation. With no swords striking or still drawn against them, Tyranos walked casually through the camp to see what they had captured. Panothos approached with Gyttja and the palace girls from the opposite side of the camp, meeting no resistance.

The Greeks began the task of finishing off the wounded, of which there were not many. Most of the students had retreated into the wood line and run past Panothos' scouts in such a frenzy that they didn't even notice the scouts spying inside the shifting morning shadows.

A victory like this was sterile and easily achieved chiefly due to the inexperience of the trainees and the total surprise waged by the attackers. The child soldiers had tried to form defensive lines but were far too off-balance to react in concert with one another. The small garrison had dispersed in chaos, bleeding and terrified, as they ran screaming into the thick evergreen forest.

The student officers and commanders who had tried to resist were immediately cut down before the Greeks were even winded. The battle was brief and almost sad in nature; it was over in minutes, and many of the fallen were only mere teens. Spartan military tactics and brutality dominated the skirmish and easily won the morning. The Greeks had only suffered a few cuts and bruises.

No honor was lost in annihilating these child soldiers; they were obstacles that had to be cleared for their plan to move forward and an escape to be realized. If these had been hardened troops, the tables most likely would have turned in the opposite direction, rendering the escape attempt a complete failure before it ever took flight.

Immediately, Tyranos and a few of his men raided the small armory in the center of the camp, securing even more swords, spears, and scraps to make shields, even finding a few bows and some quivers of arrows. Panothos and the girls went straight for the stables at the fortification's rear, which they had spotted just before laying siege on the unsuspecting garrison. They gathered up all the horses and as much feed as they could carry, packing it all for rough terrain. The men found tables of freshly baked flatbreads that had just been made to feed the soldiers after their morning rouse.

Today, the blessings of the gods were clearly on the side of the men and the servant girls. They finished grabbing any resources they could carry: blankets, cooking utensils, olive oil, dried beans, scrolls, anything to make their escape successful. They rode hastily from the site, moving defiantly forward, now possessing armor and weapons, riding on decent mounts, with food to eat and a real chance at surviving the rest of the day in one piece.

They had besieged a poorly defended outpost with stones, slings, and bedsheets for weaponry. Panothos thought that the odds of survival had begun turning in their favor. Ten hours earlier, he had thought that at least it would be a quick death attempting such a radical maneuver so deeply embedded in Persian territory. This small victory instilled hope in the hearts of the escapees. There was no stopping them; momentum was building with each step they took, traveling further away from captivity.

The group pushed forward daringly; they were now rewarded and reinvigorated with the prospect of a new life. After looking through the scrolls and maps, Panothos, an impressive strategist, could clearly see his immediate direction. The group would move north up the river for an hour, then make the tactically illogical pivot, going even more due north into the Zagros Mountains, away from Greece and their homelands.

If they managed to survive this first very challenging ascent, they would go directly into what seemed another impossible situation, escaping through a much more significant obstacle ... the Caucasus. This would "not" be the path of least resistance by any stretch of thinking; quite the contrary, it was the path of most resistance.

It was also the best place to gain the tactical advantage of taking the high ground and strategically picking their battlefield. He understood that the Persian forces who would follow assumed the group was scared and running for their lives, not planning and attempting a counter-offensive. By taking the high ground, they might be able to fight off a much larger advancing force with proper defensive positioning and synchronized responses.

He knew that up in the mountain trails, there would be many places to hide and effectively set up an ambush. Though it is harsh for both sides, the chased and the pursuer, the one in place first on the high ground has the asymmetrical advantage by attempting to dictate the time, place, and footing.

Finally, they pivoted into two columns, then split again into a third, leaving so many tracks that might confuse their pursuers, causing them to slow their progress for a while. Any of even the slightest advantages would be a welcome addition to Panothos' strategy.

They rode wildly on both sides of the riverbank, crisscrossing through the foliage until they came to the pass that would lead them up into the mountains, attempting to confuse the pursuers of their chosen route. Now, they would attempt what looked to be a harrowing ascent on what was shown on the map as a simple mountain trail, but up close, it barely looked like a path.

From the base of the trail, the mountain stood like an angry God imposing his will on the surrounding countryside. Dark clouds partially covered its highest peaks, and winds whipped up its cavernous face. It was an inhospitable place where everything at a particular elevation turned the color of gray mud; it was cracked and layered with minerals and hidden crevices throughout.

As they ascended, the trails scribed on the maps they had confiscated earlier from the training camp became more apparent. Though spice traders and goats used these routes, the paths were not worn nor accommodating to horse hooves or military formations. Rocks slipped beneath their mounts' feet and rolled down the sides of the cliff walls, causing more rocks to give way and tumble down. The Spartans were accustomed to mountain warfare and were trained at elevation to use the terrain to their advantage; they knew how to navigate these harsh conditions.

The small rocks cascading down the slope could be triggered almost at will, and if triggered at just the right time, they could be used as a powerfully devastating weapon. The path's sometimes narrow and limited footing could be used as a funnel for flanking an off-balance foe. This might then hide the weakness and size of their own contingent while keeping the more significant force's movements compressed to a small area, just as was the case in the last bloody battle that bought them the time needed for their population to regroup in the rear. This would prove vital in stifling the uphill progress of their pursuers. The tactic had held off the majority of Persian advances at Thermopylae until they were ultimately outflanked and vastly outnumbered.

This time, Panothos would try desperately to avoid repeating the same outcome as the last.

Chapter 4

Down Into the Vortex

Samid and his men gave chase in a desperate forward lunge, driving their horses almost as if they were the ones being pursued. They rode through the valley with the glaring sun rising at their backs, only stopping occasionally to let the horses rest and let the trackers verify the direction of the group's escape.

Their trail was barely evident, but to the Persians' advantage, a light dew had set in on the grass the night before and had yet to burn off. By the process of elimination, one could tell all the directions that the prisoners had not advanced. It appeared they were going towards the small cavalry training camp just before the mountain pass to the north.

Samid thought it strange that the prisoners were not headed exactly due west in the direction of Greece but rather to the north into the high mountains and places sane men had no business. He wondered exactly how these men would know the lay of the Persian lands, or were they just flying blindly in the path of least resistance? One option of escape that offered itself to common sense would be to evade capture by traversing unoccupied lands.

The other option was to try and blend in with the local populations and move slowly and tread lightly, possibly moving on the spice trail through the tribal territories in the arid regions on the way to Greece. Military outposts were well hidden in those mountain villages, and a few small occupied cities under Persian control were scattered along the spice trail. Samid assumed that the Spartan pride and bravado would keep them from creeping down the southern spice trail. He wagered that the Spartans had taken the more brutal option and first headed north.

As the first column of Samid's men approached the mountain pass, they saw smoke rising from the valley with the training camp; two forward trackers hurried to the rear of the column with a couple of the terrified boys in tow. They picked the boys up hiding behind some brush in the wooded area beside the trail. When they reached Samid's position, guards immediately forced the two boys to their knees.

One of the boys began begging Samid for mercy and pleading for forgiveness as he told the harrowing story of the morning raid they had endured. He exclaimed that most of the student soldiers were fleeing into the forest, and the instructors and older boys put up a suicidal resistance, fighting off the massive army of invaders. With every last drop of blood, they fought where they stood and died defending themselves from these professional killers. Samid's face blazed red; he was infuriated. *The lies this boy spews to try to save himself.* He knew there was no "large army," that only the escaped prisoners and some slave girls had come through a Persian camp and laid waste to it, and in the middle of their homeland no less ... and on the outskirts of the holy city!

Samid, screaming at the top of his lungs at the boys, told them to bow their heads in shame, and pray for forgiveness. The boys, now crying, did precisely as he ordered: kneeling, praying ... all the while sobbing and blubbering uncontrollably. He looked at his men with a scowl, shaking his head, and silently nodded. He rode off to join back up with the main body of the column.

Raza Douul was furious at his overnight guards for letting this happen and knew precisely what Samid's disgust was. He dismounted his horse, drew his heavy scimitar from its curved hilt, and drove it down onto the first soldier's neck with vicious impunity. His head rolled onto the roadside, and his body emptied its dark red fluids into the starving Persian soil. The scene repeated as the second boy's body flailed like a fish out of water, bouncing around from the disconnection of his head from its spinal column. The soldiers looked on in horror, contemplating what fate may await them if they did not find the escapees soon enough. A few of the men retched from the sight, drawing Raza Douul's disapproving stare.

As the column moved forward, this scene repeated with the young soldiers until they arrived at the training camp where the attack had occurred. Smoke rose into the sky and fires smoldered from where the Greeks had torched the tents and small buildings. When Raza Douul told Samid what was missing from the camp's inventory, Samid's temper went on full display to his men's detriment. *The Greeks now have swords, maps, and horses!*

He was livid, getting right up in Raza Douul's face, repeatedly spitting and poking his fingers into his chest! He then railed at his men, "Remember the faces of each of the decapitated men and realize ... this is also going to be your fate if you don't hurry up and capture these vermin; they are now armed and running roughshod through our homeland completely unabated! Now move!"

He walked back and mounted his horse, then ordered his troops up the trail in double time. It seemed to him that he was the only one with a spine who sought a victory today. He knew that time was not on his side and a triumph must be swift to appease his king. This group of injured prisoners would not make him look like a fool again.

Panothos was advancing steadily up the mountain pass; he dismounted his horse and stared deep down into the distant valley floor. It was a tapestry of dry green and brown foliage, somewhat like his homeland's arid mountains and rich valleys for which he painfully yearned.

Massive, sprawling trees shaded the meadows in the lower valley, casting shadows and offering a measurement of time and distance. He could read the time of day by the pitch of the shadow objects cast. He could roughly judge the distance by the size he now saw the trees. He exclaimed to Aurias, "Here is the place to get free of these pursuers!"

Aurias showed his approval with a nod, replying, "I agree; this feels like a place where the impatient come to die!"

The Greeks spread out at Panothos' orders and began exploring and digging into the area. His chosen fighting position was on a plateau just above the most challenging part of the trail's ascent they had encountered thus far. Traversing this section of the trail would be no more unobstructed for their pursuers than for the Greeks. Hence, as they passed through this corridor, they would have to focus on their footing instead of on the silent, entrenched killers waiting somewhere on the narrow path, ready to destroy them. Panothos held the high ground on this mountain, at least for the moment ... in a place that closely resembled the hot gates of Thermopylae.

Boulders littered the tight chasm, allowing only three or four men on horseback to zigzag through the pass at one interval. Just before the chasm, there was a vast twisting corridor of uneven terrain with rock walls on both sides and more boulders inhibiting their horse's footing; this would be where the Persians would bunch up, waiting to push through the narrow winding gap. This was where Panothos would make his stand against the pursuing Persian cavalry and where the tempered fate of the newly free men of Greece would ultimately be challenged.

It was late in the day, and the sun was slowly setting over the vast horizon, leaving the weightless clouds wafting in the blue sky; they seemed to burn with jagged, fiery orange streaks and cascading sunbeams. The mountain's towering face, backlit in silhouette, towered over the plush valley floor.

Samid gazed at the peak of the Goliath, with its jagged switchbacks folding in and out on themselves. He thought it unwise to head into these mountains just before dark and risk splitting his force into smaller groups, losing the advantage of his power in numbers. He ordered the men to camp to prepare for an early morning ascent.

When Panothos' rear scouts returned with the news that the pursuers had stopped their advance and made camp, he could finally take a moment to breathe and devise a much more precise battle plan to survive the upcoming onslaught. He knew he could not keep pace with the advancing force, and he knew the odds were not in his favor, but the sheer hubris of his team gave him faith that they stood a real chance of surviving the impending assault.

He again sent scouts forward to find the best escape paths through the mountain passes, leaving lookouts back in the rear to warn of any attempted movements the Persians may try and aim at them in stealth. In opposition, the Persians set up sentries around their temporary encampment and sent scouts up to the second switchback in the climb, just an hour's hike short of the narrow pass.

The Greek lookouts attempted to collect intelligence on exactly what type of force they would encounter in their inevitable collision. Gaining an intimate knowledge of your adversary was a skill that Spartan warriors excelled at thoroughly. They knew that one of the Persian war machine's greatest strengths was their siege weapons, which would wear down a fortress' defenses until the main body of their forces could penetrate the weakest point and enter its walls.

Heavy siege machines were a burdensome nuisance in these dense mountains and something to be painstakingly hauled around and maintained.

They did not lend themselves to these guerrilla warfare conditions. Samid could not utilize these heavy siege weapons for this occasion; they were useless to his cause. He opted instead for a light cavalry force, reducing the Persian effectiveness, but it made the most sense for the rough terrain and the splintered, crude type of resistance they might face.

Samid was utterly infuriated that his men had not recaptured the escapees already on day one after the festival. He wanted to relish the honor of victory heaped upon him from a vast adoring public still in a celebratory mood. His blood boiled, and his anger smoldered unquenched, keeping him awake for most of the long night, planning the assault in his head.

He repeatedly second-guessed Raza Douul's actions in the pursuit thus far, searching for any small thing, any reason to blame and pick at those in lesser positions whose weakness, in his estimation, had failed to bring him the instant results he so craved. His men, also in grave fear for their own lives, didn't sleep that evening; they knew the temper of their master, and with dread their only proper incentive, rest seemed a luxury.

The Persian soldiers were also playing out all the scenarios of the impending battle in their wildly racing minds: what the last moment must feel like when the sword starts cutting through your hair, skin, and neck. Would their families ever learn of their demise? The primal fear of meeting a legendary Spartan warrior in face-to-face combat intimidated these young men. From any angle one looked at the situation, the inescapable outcome was utterly terrifying. The only possible way to survive the coming day was littered with fever-pitched dreams and a seared mental image of unwaveringly shocking violence.

In the Spartan camp, the men snored loudly throughout the night and rested for the challenging day ahead. Night sentries were placed to make sure there were no incursions into their defensive position; the men would go so far as to lean against their sword tips to avoid falling asleep while on watch.

During the day's ascent, one of the stolen horses broke its leg on loose stones coming up through the narrow pass; it was an older mount, a breeding stud, and it had to be put down due to this grave injury. The Greeks butchered it and roasted it on their spear tips over small fires in a makeshift covered pit of stacked stones just inside an empty bear cave they found in the cliff face.

They feasted on the tenderloin, liver, heart, and the stolen flatbread they gathered from the enemy camp that morning. All the men ate until their bellies were full. They really felt like soldiers again, free again, in command of their own destiny, bracing for whatever hardships the coming day would pummel them with. For all they knew, it would be the last warm meal they might ever eat. The meat, though chewy, tasted divine, even without any herbs or garlic.

The odds were stacked against them; the terrain was atrocious, their injuries left them vulnerable, and their numbers were few, but their focus and resolve were crystalline: do or die, and if it were to be death, a glorious death in battle they would seek.

Panothos rose early in the morning to meet his fate, far before the sun would rise to chase away the escaping shades of night's cover. He stretched his stiff and aching body before the other warriors stirred. He looked over at the girls; Gyttja was also awake, watching Panothos do his stretches in the pale pre-dawn light. She spoke not a single word, but Panothos felt her presence shining above the moment.

When she noticed Panothos had stopped stretching and was looking squarely back at her, she rose nervously, blushing, and quickly began to rouse the other girls, almost as if she were embarrassed that he had caught her watching him for so long. Panothos then awoke his men, mustering them into a huddle. Once they were all awake and perfectly alert, he began to bark the morning's orders to the men, encouraging them to bravely face the enormity of the tasks ahead. The rear scouts rushed up just as the morning light finally broke free of the mountain's silhouette; they relayed to him that it was the scenario all the men must have dreamed of all evening.

"Sir, the whole of the Persian force marches up the trail directly to our current position, dispersed in three columns!" Panothos discreetly reveled in the news. The Persian force's formation was a textbook conventional military formation used in phase-line warfare; it was simply not meant for asymmetrical close-quarter mountain combat, which was precisely how Panothos intended to repel the sizeable pursuing force. He spoke to the group to calm their nerves and focus them on the task at hand.

"My friends, my brothers, here we are at our world's edge … At this place and time, we have chosen to stand and meet our destiny head-on, with our eyes open wide, staring willfully forward … to a future free from this tyrant's chains! You already know what it will take to defeat our pursuers; only a brave heart and a will of iron will earn back our freedom. Though we face these great odds that have been once again thrust upon us, our fate is not beyond our control. Because of who we are, we shall be triumphant!

"With all the blood that is left pumping in our veins and the untamed spirit in our hearts, we will rise to embrace our fate eagerly!

"Are you with me?"

The group raised their swords and spears in the air and let out a resounding "HWOU!" while beating once on their chests in unanimous approval.

They rapidly dispersed into the mountain pass, crawling onto cliffs and into crevices to take up their positions. The warriors situated themselves in pairs, staggering incrementally in between the rock outcroppings that dotted the upper trail. Trusting in Panothos' logic, they crouched silently, hidden by the leading edge of the rocks that protruded just above the narrow trail's opening.

Earlier in the morning, hours before the sun rose, the rear scouts returning from their reconnaissance mission littered the chasm with the shredded guts of the slain horse from the night's feast. They generously soaked the pathway in its coagulating blood, feces, bile, and splintered bones. They knew that sometimes the psychology before a battle determines the outcome more than the action of the actual fighting itself. You could stoke their fear if you knew what men's imagination dreaded the most. If you make your enemy truly fear you, they will be consumed by the malignance of their underlying trepidation.

As the sun rose, Samid's anxious men began ascending the treacherous winding pass agitatedly, with so much fear in their hearts that it made them even more careless than they would typically be. Samid, with his elite guard, brought up the rear of the outstretched column.

As the leading group of horsemen in the Persian advance began to reach the chasm, the Greek forward positions could hear the soldiers groaning in disgust from the gruesome decorations splattered about on the cliff face. Entrails and feces decorated the approach like some unusual sacrificial tribute.

Men could be heard vomiting from the stench of the bile and blood flung around and left to go foul on the rock walls. Thousands of flies buzzed and crawled all over and around the men's uncovered faces, aggravating them incessantly. This, coupled with the elevation, became a nuisance that made them lose focus on what might be waiting for them in the shadows.

The Greeks waited ever so still, patiently watching the oncoming soldiers advancing slowly up the trail until well past their positions. The plan was to let half the men through the chasm, only then unleashing an attack.

The Persian soldiers never imagined that the Greeks would have made camp so close to their own on the previous night. Samid figured they had probably summited the mountain and made camp somewhere over the peak to get as far away as possible before his forces could catch up with them; now they moved in double time to catch up with their scurrying prey.

Panothos split his men into three groups. The first group was to attack the forward advance at the chasm. The next was to attack a small plateau where the enemy would stack up, waiting to pass through. Then he sent three Greek soldiers with the rest of the horses further up the pass, away from the Persians and Persepolis as if they were hastily fleeing up the trail. They carried bundles of smoldering dung on their backs. The smoldering dung was wrapped in wet moss and fresh evergreen boughs. The smoke from the bundles rose into the morning sky like steam billowing in the wind. From this, you could tell the path of the escaping horses from far down the mountain grade.

The first third of the Persian force split up and went ahead of the rest of the column, triggered into pursuit by the dust trail of the most likely evacuating prisoners. Raza Douul very clearly stated the standing orders from their leader. They were to wait for Samid's column and the rear guard to approach and converge with them before progressing further up the trail and making contact.

In the early morning light, Kaveh, a cocky young Persian cavalry officer at the front of the group, saw the dust rising in the air so close to him that he wanted to steal the victory away from his counterparts in the other two groups. He knew in his heart that a quick success would elevate him in the ranks and help him to find favor with Samid. Thinking he had them firmly in his grasp, he completely ignored his orders, immediately breaking stride and ordering his team to pursue the escaping prisoners down the trail.

Now well past the bloody, gut-filled chasm, his whole team took to a full gallop and put the space of his whole division between them and the formations of the horsemen that followed. Panothos waited patiently as the next group carefully navigated into the chasm; the Greeks could hear the middle cavalry procession lunging forward impatiently to catch up with the first group which had disobeyed orders and were now in full heated pursuit. They gagged and groaned as soon as they were tightly packed in the small canyon, advancing through its uneven surfaces, trying not to touch the mess on the narrow walls. Only when Samid and his rear guard entered halfway into the bloody kill box did Panothos call for the attack to commence.

Two flaming arrows arched high into the morning air. This was Panothos' cue for the soldiers at the entrance of the chasm to start pushing rocks down into the gap, creating cascading rockslides and damming up the pass. The rocks tumbled violently down the cliff face.

Above the chasm entrance, the girls lit massive round bales of grass and twigs laden with horse fat and grease drippings. Bound by the ligaments of the meat they had eaten the night before, they pushed the burning bundles down the steep slope above the chasm ... It had been a lean meal the night before because all the fats and marrow were rendered to make flammable oil.

The balls of flaming debris engulfed the path just behind Samid and his guard; it spooked the horses, causing some of them to lunge forward, wedging them into the last portions of the second column, drastically overcrowding the very narrow mountain trail exactly as Panothos had envisioned. The team rolled rocks down the hill, then broke off and ran down the switchback to attack the front side of the second column. They moved far up the trail to draw the second column out of their form further.

As the loose rocks continued to tumble down onto the trail, the horses from the rear pushed forward desperately to get away from the expanding flames and smoke behind them. The remaining Greeks, led by Tyranos, attacked with a vicious assault on the second group of soldiers, who had already made their way through the pass.

They advanced on the Persians with a lethal wall of spears, which they had carved and sharpened in the fire the night before while dining on the horse meat. They reached a skirmish line and planted the base of their spears in the dirt, pointing in the direction of the oncoming front.

Twenty or so horses got spooked and galloped rapidly forward, trying to squeeze into the narrow pass. The riders, now entirely off-balance from the ambush, were trying to gain control of them but only did so as they ran up on Tyranos' impalement line just as it raised the spears from the dirt to greet them violently.

Some of the horses rammed themselves into the sharp spears and rose into the air and backward before crashing down on top of their riders. The Greeks in the third line stabbed at the men approaching, and the second line of men stabbed the ones who had fallen off their horses; they performed like a killing machine, in step, lunging steadily and methodically.

On the Persian side of the battle line, horses were bucking and collapsing, their legs breaking as boulders kept coming down, gaining tremendous momentum, taking whole shelves of the hill down the steep grade and into the chasm.

Men were being crushed by rocks and trampled to death by the terrified horses in the back. Spears came from the front, rocks slid from the side, and fire and chaos decimated the formation from the rear.

Samid looked on in absolute horror as his combat unit rapidly unraveled before his very eyes. *Have my men no shame?* he thought to himself.

A group of supposedly weak, wounded prisoners and slaves quickly annihilated the attacking force, crushing them into the ground with sticks and stones right before his eyes. He began barking orders and trying to get his men back to rally into some formation. But it was too late; the damage had been done. The corridor was littered with dead oxen and wounded horses, large rocks, and soldiers battling to the death in the narrow space left in the front line.

The chasm was made virtually impassable from all the bodies and boulders stacking up, and to make matters worse, they were running panicked into a Spartan phalanx head-on. Samid's men had split up and disobeyed his orders, halving the size of his forces and spreading them into unmanageable positions. There was no choice but to dismount and try to get close to the skirmish line on foot.

He yelled to his men, "Dismount and attack!" He followed behind, pushing and crawling over the dead and injured horses and mangled bleeding corpses of his men. He finally reached a place to stand up and take stock of the situation ... He rose to see if there was any way to salvage this horrible tactical blunder. Still, he could only look on in disbelief at the ever-evolving situation, which was beginning to look very bleak indeed.

As the Greeks attacked at the chasm, the three horsemen in the front team stopped and took the smoking dung bundles off the horses' backs. They ran down a small trail and dropped the bundles off a cliff face at the end of the trail; it was a loose rocky pass, a densely covered game trail that led to a blind ledge that only a mountain goat could manage to get down without plummeting to its death.

One of the Greek scouts had almost lost his footing the night before doing the reconnaissance mission; he found it a dead end. He almost slid off the cliff due to his momentum but caught some roots just before he went over the edge. He thought it a natural weapon, and when he told Panothos, he immediately integrated it into the quickly crafted plan.

Earlier in the night, before dawn's light broke, one of the horsemen led the rest of the remaining herd further, just over the peak into a slight depression in a ravine, and hid them from the path with a makeshift wooden brush fence. The other two men hurried up around the switchback on the trail and took cover behind a huge boulder to see if their deception would lead the pursuers away.

They camouflaged the more established trail with some large rocks, and they took some shrubs from the entrance of the dangerous goat path to route the Persians down the small path instead of up the main trail where the horses were hidden. They felt the ground start to rumble as the first of the horsemen, riding at full gallop, approached from the chasm; they almost passed by the boulders and debris, but Kaveh halted abruptly, looking around inquisitively. He raised his hand in the air, and the group slowed and looked around.

Seeing the smoke so far down the trail, one of the men pointed out a dust cloud at the bottom of the smaller overgrown trail leading down in the same direction. Kaveh bought the diversion in the heat of the chase and decided to charge down the sparse goat trail. Evergreen branches were smacking them in the eyes and face as they rode unwisely down the path. Rocks began breaking loose and sliding under the horses' hooves; a smokey haze had started to build up in the area from the smoldering bundles bellowing below. An acrid smoke burned their eyes intensely, making them watery and blurring the riders' vision.

The horses were hesitant to go down the pathway at this gallop into the fog of dust and smoke, but the Persian soldiers vengefully dug in their heels, drawing blood from the horses' sides; the horses bolted straight into the wall of haze. Kaveh, not to be outdone, pushed his beast brutishly forward. They believed they were so close to victory that they could taste the flavor of hatred in their saliva! Finally, this day would become their day of glory, and then ...

A strange silence shrouded the cliff face ...

You could only hear the horses whinnying with a hollow echoing reverberation ... then the next one, and the next one, and the next. The horses' massive bodies impacting the trail floor below made a terrible thudding noise like watermelons splitting open on sharp rocks. One after the other, they raced down to the hidden cliff face, blinded by fear and rage, compounded by evergreen sap and dung smoke.

All the riders tried to pull back on the reins at the last second and stop when they approached the ledge but were pushed off by the momentum of the one just behind them in a cruel chain reaction. They just kept going over until the last of the first column of Kaveh's riders followed them over the ledge; like cliff-diving lemmings they went, losing control of their steeds, hooves sliding in the loose gravel.

Today, their rabid bloodlust and fear of Samid was so great that they unknowingly jumped their horses into the abyss, into a characterless death, just a greedy and foolish blind leap.

Simultaneously, Tyranos seized the upper hand in the battle against the second column's advance in the bloody chasm. He and Aurias were spearheading the counter-offensive with great success. Seeing the possibility of a total routing defeat, Samid and his remaining rear guard retreated hastily back down the mountain pass from which they came. As the horses plunged through the burning straw bundles on the trail going down the mountain, you could smell their manes being singed and hear the terrified screams of the men passing through the gauntlet.

Samid, before today, had only known one-sided victories. Now, at the hand of these very few ingrates, he had suffered a crushing defeat and could only imagine his fate when Xerxes learned that he had let escape his favored prize! He angrily cursed this day, whipping his mount to get as far away from the carnage as possible.

He looked over his shoulder to see how many of his men had taken notice of the order to retreat, but they did not follow him in droves; only a few of the rear guards trickled out of the chasm. Raza Douul and most of the men were now on foot, injured, climbing over the bodies that littered the only pathway back down the rugged mountain; they were all trying desperately to run to the rally point where the others eagerly retreated with Samid.

As the golden sun began to pass high over the shifting colors of the jagged mountain peaks and the haze of the battle began to wane, three of the Greeks and two of the palace girls lay dead on the trail, with almost eighty or so of the Persian guards. Panothos was amazed at the tenacity of his fallen soldiers and the raw vigor and strength of the servant girls. They had died with honor and shown incredible bravery in the face of the ferocious attack.

The bodies of the men and the girls were placed onto a pyre and lit; soon the flames illuminated the early evening sky and could be seen from the valley floor by Samid's retreating forces. There would be no victory celebration this evening; escape was the priority and the more space they could put between them and Xerxes' forces, the better off they would ultimately be.

The Greeks slowly descended the north side of the mountain range carefully under cover of night. They headed for the flats around a large body of water they could see from the higher elevation in the distance. As Panothos and the others descended the trail, they passed where the careless Persian cavalry had gone over the mountain ledge. The sight of men and beasts mangled together was unlike anything they had ever witnessed, even in the fiercest battles.

It punctuated the intensity Xerxes' men would bring to the chase and the ferocity of their determination to recapture them. With Samid now in retreat, Panothos knew Xerxes would double his efforts to reclaim his so-called Spartan "trophies." Now, at least, the Persians had to find the Greeks again, which may be more challenging next time, just as long as Panothos could quickly distance the party from their Persian pursuers.

Panothos kept a steady pace due north once firmly past the mountain range. He sent three men to the west with some of the horses; he loaded them down with extra weight so they would forge a blatant and obvious trail due west, back up into the mountains towards Mother Greece. Once this team had journeyed for a day or two, they were to dump the excess weight, cover their tracks, and ride hard north easterly to rally with the lead group in the north near the furthest most edge of the lake they had spotted from the mountain peak.

One after the other, the group pushed through the nights and made camp in cave systems or hidden shaded ravines during the daylight hours, wherever they could find decent shelter. They rested and moved cautiously ever northward to the water's edge. Panothos assumed that whatever force sent to capture him would be more cautious in the future and not rush in with the same sophomoric zeal as Samid's men did. They had been fortunate thus far, and he didn't want to tempt fate with any simple missteps. One thing they had going for them was that the moon was full at night, and they could move through the darkness without torchlight.

The perilous journey to a new life and home had begun in earnest. The idea of domesticity was a new concept to the Spartan men. None had ever imagined they would be fugitives, nor did they ever dream they would be looking for a safe place to rest their bones and settle down. Tyranos and Aurias were the most concerned with this idea; they knew it was how it must be, but they were apprehensive about living a "common" life where warfare wasn't their primary objective or responsibility …

The men kept their campfires small and encampments sparse. The scouts would kill game birds that the girls would cook on the hot coals, then bury the ashes and remains in the wood line just before the sun disappeared from the horizon every evening. They pushed forward in the early evening hours just as the average peasant farmers ended their day and bedded down. The terrain was treacherous and harsh, sometimes shifting beneath their feet. It was mainly becoming desert, with flash flood washouts and wind-eroded rock formations.

Some oases had to be gone around if locals were camping near the fresh water. They would send the rear scouts back if no people were around and only then refill their sheep bladders. With a force this small, they could move without creating a large, easily trackable footprint on the land.

The soldiers in the rear did their best to cover up the trail or put out false tracks as countermeasures to confuse any trackers. Panothos would take different routes than the apparent paths to avoid accidental detection. He had taken one human prize from the training outpost on the first day of the escape, a young Persian soldier from the cartography tent. Panothos chose to take him with them rather than kill him.

The boy was blindfolded, bound, and terrified in a blubbering panic. He was drenched in fear and disgustingly filthy. He imagined he would die at any moment during the skirmish in the mountains, but Panothos guarded him personally to ensure he remained alive to serve his purpose. Though he was unaware of it, he was an asset to them, but he had no idea of his actual value.

After the battle with Samid, Tyranos grabbed the young man, pulled him close to his face, pulled the blindfold down, and told the boy, "Now, the decisions you make will determine how long you live in this world! You will tell us how to escape from this wretched desert, boy!" The Persian fell quickly to his knees and started begging desperately for Tyranos to spare his life.

He had heard stories of the Spartans and how ruthless they were in battle, but more so, he feared being recaptured by Xerxes' bloodthirsty and egomaniacal officers. He knew that defeat or capture would lead him to a hideous and painful death; an example would be made of him before the other conscripts.

One of the girls translated what he said back to Tyranos. He pleaded with him to spare his young life. He tried to explain to him that he would try to guide them through the remainder of these lands on the maps safely; he would be a loyal and trustworthy slave as it was his only choice. "On my mother's life!" he promised repeatedly. "I will do my best to keep you away from Persian outposts!"

Tyranos shook his head in disgust and yelled at the boy, "Where is your spine? Do you possess any honor inside yourself at all?

"You are a disgrace of a human to show allegiance to us Greeks. We are your sworn enemies!

"I should slay you right here where you stand for being such a groveling Persian pig!"

The boy trembled in the face of such overt hostility! He turned pale and began shaking; fresh urine wet his trousers, which had already reeked from him pissing himself during the battle at the first outpost.

Tyranos laughed and then curled up the corner of his lip in disgust, spitting into the dust at his feet. The boy knew he was damned if he did or did not help them.

"Oh, this cruel purgatory ... it is a fate worse than death!" he mumbled to himself.

The servant girl Sigrun, seeing the fear in the shaking boy, grabbed him and scowled at Tyranos with foreign words he couldn't understand, but her tone he understood perfectly. She called Tyranos a rabid animal and put her arm around the scared boy, pulling him away from his aggressor and wiping his face.

Sigrun and another servant girl took the boy to the side and out of Tyranos' path to clean up the frightened boy. She asked Sigrun, "Why do you tempt Tyranos' anger?"

Sigrun scowled, "He just intimidates him for sport. The boy has had enough torment; it is plain to see he is scared out of his wits.

"This brutality can gain nothing; the boy is now only trying to help us. He was probably sold into this life. To treat him with such cruelty makes us no better than our pursuer."

The servant Aesa nodded; she was the youngest and newest of the palace girls from the north. Frightened in her own right, she completely understood Sigrun's compassion for the scared boy. She, too, had been thrust into a life of servitude. Here, out in the wilds, she was learning to be a woman from brave women facing incredible adversity.

Panothos approached, walking unknowingly into this tense situation. Upon hearing the commotion, the next best move was to diffuse the tension, reassure the boy that he would come to no harm, and pacify Sigrun with less abrasive words.

He spoke to Tyranos calmly in his native tongue, "Tyranos, my dear friend ... I feel as you do. I wish to slaughter every last one of these Persian vermin, but remember this one has a purpose; I chose to let him live for a reason, to serve our needs while we remain in Persian-controlled lands."

Tyranos replied, "Panothos, I trust in your judgment, but I do not trust this worm not to lead us into an ambush. He has no honor; how can we trust a man who has no honor? ... He is just a rat, driven by his desire to persist!"

Panothos nodded in agreement. "For now, you must trust in my decision to let him remain alive. He will be useful at some point, I can just feel it in my bones; call it a premonition."

Tyranos walked away, shaking his head in disapproval, cutting his eyes at Sigrun, then went to speak with Aurias, who toiled with the horses, feeding them grain to keep up their strength and removing some of the plates of armor from their saddles and chest plates. Panothos asked Sigrun to tell the boy that he would be well taken care of if he showed them the way out of the Persian territories and never disobeyed their orders; then, he would be truly free from this nightmare.

Panothos asked the boy his name ...

"Ashkan," he spoke, crying and trembling. "My name is Ashkan ..."

Panothos nodded and slowly squatted, balancing himself with a spear that he planted into the soil before the boy. He told the young man, "You must take us to the north where these girls hail from!" Sigrun translated his words.

Ashkan nodded his head and thanked Panothos repeatedly.

The girls had been captive long enough to communicate accurately with the boy in his native tongue. In broken pieces of three different languages, they devised a direction on the maps and a plan to move steadily to the north, far away from the greater Persian Empire. At this point, they were a small enough group that could still avoid drawing too much attention from the public, but still a large enough force to take out sentries or a small, garrisoned guard force. They were dangerous enough to have a real fighting chance at survival now, and Panothos would not give in without giving every last spark of energy he had left in his aching bones.

Chapter 5

The Slow Death of a Spider

After many harrowing days of travel, the second decoy group returned with the horses, finally arriving in a lush area with fruit trees near the outskirts of a small, ancient, abandoned settlement. The many days in the desert hills had taken a severe toll on the men and animals, so Panothos, taking Gyttja's advice, decided now would be a perfect time and place to rest and hunt. They would strategize and reorganize for the next phase of their escape on the high trail through the mountains.

On the other side of a dense forest, the scouts came across another large mass of brackish water. Some of the men and a few girls went with the scouts to prepare for the road ahead. They helped make small improvised boats to survey the area quickly and also to try and net some fish; they would need the protein for the next leg of the journey. Once through the trees and on the water, the horizon opened up, and the scouts saw a vast, ominous mountain range that rose high into the air, defining the horizon.

The Caucasus Mountains pierced menacingly into the clouds like a cluster of towering castles that seemed to stretch forever. Seemingly put there as a barrier that only served the gods, not at all a place fit for men to dwell.

Panothos and Demetrios, with Ashkan in tow, forged ahead on the trail to do some reconnaissance. They crept up on a small settlement nestled in the western foothills as the rest of Panothos' people fished and foraged near the camp. He decided to enter this village with Ashkan and see if they could collect any valuable intelligence from the local tribesmen. Had this village heard of the group of escaped prisoners, or were they far enough away from Persepolis to not draw attention to themselves?

When Panothos and Ashkan entered the village, they were greeted by hordes of children begging for food and coins in the streets. A guard force of Persian sentries who seemed oblivious to the two men's shabby presence looked right past them and into the distance as they passed by; their current state of filth perfectly obscured them after so many days traveling in the desert.

They were both sun-drenched and wearing badly dirt-stained clothes. Panothos was beginning to resemble an impoverished local peasant, which he suspected may help to conceal them. When a vendor in the bazaar or sentry would speak to them, Ashkan would step in and tell them that his companion was a salt trader who had been robbed by bandits in the foothills but was born a mute and could not answer their questions. Panothos nodded and grunted when spoken to, but it seemed for the moment that none of the villagers or sentries were wise to him being one of the fugitive prisoners.

They walked carefully through the village bazaar, trading some small animal pelts for flatbreads to return to the camp. They hid the items underneath their garments to avoid attracting unwanted attention. They went inside the village center to sit, have tea, and see if the area was a threat.

Then, as feared, posted right in the center of the village on a wall in the square right next to the tea stall, was an alarming scroll that Ashkan translated to Panothos in broken bits of Greek. It offered a large reward for the escaped fugitives. It was vague in its description of them, but still, they were not far enough away to relax their guard.

Panothos knew the Persians were more advanced than most, but he could not imagine the news of their escape would be posted in a remote village near the empire's borderlands; it made his skin tingle and put him on high alert. They were moving up the trail at a decent pace. He surmised that the Persians could get ahead of them on the water, solidifying his plan to traverse the mountain passes for the next leg of the journey; otherwise, the Persians would surely wedge them between the mountains and the water. With no place to exit and no way to outrun them, they would be sitting ducks, pinched into defending three fronts of their enemy's choosing.

Leaving his cloak pulled close to his face to avoid detection, he scanned the surrounding alleys and teahouses when a peculiar sight caught his attention. A woman sitting at a table across the square, wearing a black scarf, was staring at the two of them out of the corner of her eye. She seemed to be paying far too much attention to them and looked as if she were going out of her way not to look in their direction for more than a glance at a time.

Panothos and Ashkan finished their tea and left the square, heading through the bazaar and down some uneven stone steps into a dark, twisting alleyway. A slick patch of algae formed in the gutter channel of the steps, which Ashkan nearly slipped on before Panothos grabbed him by the arm, keeping him from falling.

They ducked into an unoccupied, crumbling, mud-brick abandoned storehouse, moving in the dark. After a few minutes, the veiled woman followed cautiously down the corridor and into the same entrance, almost slipping on the algae. Panothos crouched and hid behind an old wooden crate left inside the room. Ashkan stood in the far corner of the room with his back turned, looking out of a window in plain sight, hoping to draw her attention to him first.

She crept quietly like an assassin into the room where Panothos now lay in wait, hiding in the shadows, ready to pounce. She looked around and saw Ashkan silhouetted, standing in the corner; she quickly approached him, leaving her back exposed to the entrance.

Panothos, following in her steps, crept up silently behind the woman and quickly pulled her down with his hand over her mouth, forcing her to the ground with a small dagger to her throat. She was strong; she didn't go down easily. Her eyes were wide with a look of surprise and terror.

He grunted, instructing Ashkan to ask her why she was lurking around behind them in the dark. He crudely translated the woman's words back to Panothos. She told Ashkan she was just curious as to why they were paying so much attention to her while having their tea, nothing more. Panothos grunted again. Ashkan raised his tone, "Why do you follow us?"

Panothos frisked her and found a jeweled dagger and a small bag of gold Persian coins with Xerxes' stamp pressed into them under her layered robe. As he ran his hands over her torso, searching, he could feel that she was all muscle, having a very solid physic, not the build of a typical village girl. *What a waste of beauty*, he thought to himself.

He forcefully ripped her robe open, exposing a tattoo on her right shoulder; he had seen this tattoo before at Thermopylae. It was the same insignia that the Persian shock troops wore on their chests, the soldiers who were known as "Immortals." They were supposed to be the most well-trained professional shock troops in the Persian Empire's arsenal.

Panothos knew the mark well enough ... that of a cold-hearted killer, a professional assassin. He had killed so many of these "Immortals" and wasn't impressed by their skills. They were only capable of witchcraft at best; a marriage of alchemy and hatred spun into their arsenal.

She was built like a goddess and was as beautiful as any Persian woman he had ever seen. But with this tattoo, he knew she was as cunning and deadly as a poison asp, and he had never before heard tales of a female Immortal; this was something he did not expect. Furthermore, as an Immortal, she was imbued with an unrepentant murderous focus to get close to and kill her prey by any means necessary.

Ashkan asked the assassin, "How did you find us?"

Knowing her cover was blown, she spit in his face and stared back at him, speaking in Persian with a look of pure hate.

"Why are you helping these pigs? Have they paid you? How many coins did it take for you to forsake your king and country?"

Panothos repeated the phrase and squeezed her neck until she couldn't breathe. She struggled but remained silent this time. Though strong, she was no match for a man the size of Panothos. He loosened his grip and motioned to Ashkan to ask again …

"How did you find us?"

She replied, "I just followed your foul stench."

Ashkan tried to translate her words roughly, but Panothos understood her tone well enough; she was saying something caustic to the boy. Panothos raised his hand and repeatedly bashed her in the face with his clenched fist, bouncing her head off the dusty floorboards. Blood ran from her mouth and nose, her lips now wet and dark red; it looked almost ornamentally painted on. She defiantly spat the blood and saliva back into Panothos' face. He lifted his arm high into the stale air and pummeled her with his elbow twice more. This time, he knocked her completely unconscious.

Ashkan was shaken at how quickly and without a second thought Panothos had become so violent; without hesitation or any contemplation, he had pummeled her unflinchingly … and did this to a beautiful woman, no less!

Panothos and Ashkan wrapped the now swollen-faced woman back inside her garments, then stealthily hauled her through a back alley and down to a small dry creek bed just beneath the village. Demetrios waited with the horses in a ravine around the corner in the brush, hidden from view. They bound her hands behind her back and draped her limp body face down over the back of Panothos' horse, returning to the camp with her in tow.

When the woman awoke, Panothos' men gathered around; they looked down at her, admiring her stunning physic. She was dizzy, hot, and terribly confused. Aurias knelt and looked closely at her tattoo. It filled his heart with pure rage. He pulled out his dagger and pinched at the skin where the tattoo was scribed. He took the dagger and slowly cut the tattoo off her body. He left a bleeding crater on her once-perfect skin; she screamed in immense agony. He had killed so many of these so-called "Immortals," but he had never seen one who was not wholly disfigured and scarred ... nor ever a female version of this scourge. This one was special: a beautiful black widow, an assassin who used her sensuality to attain supremacy.

In the Persian ranks, to be female and in a cult-like military order, one must be unique, a cunning specialist capable of committing any number of atrocities. Aurias raised up, lifted his knee into the air, and stomped on her head with his foot, again bouncing it from the rocks beneath. She unsteadily tried to raise her head from the ground, but he repeated the blow. The many degrees of torturous pain she was enduring on this day instantly made her lose consciousness again.

The sun beat down heavily, slowly scorching her smooth, dark skin. Dried blood and tears had crusted on her swollen eyelids and impaired her vision. This once beautiful woman's face was cut, swollen, and caked with dirt.

She awoke, feeling an unusual tension on her torso. Tyranos and Aurias stood over her body, now suspended in the air from ropes. The joints in her shoulders and hips were burning and aching like nothing she had ever experienced. She managed to open her eyes and saw the Spartan men standing over her hovering body; she was stripped completely naked.

The men had bound her arms and legs; one side was attached to horses and the other to the base of a medium-sized sapling. The horses had been led away from the tree, elevating her body from the rocky soil that had cradled her earlier in the day.

Ashkan asked her again aggressively, "How did you find us?"

She gasped in pain, crying out in her native tongue, "To the desolate pits of the underworld with you!"

The horses snorted and took a small step forward; the tree leaned towards them under the tension. The pain was pure; it was unlike anything she had ever imagined. All she could think of as she slipped back into unconsciousness was playing with her sisters in the orchards as a child. It was a kind and gentle place in a garden with fresh fig, olive, and lemon trees. A gentle breeze blew, and the tree limbs swayed in the morning sunshine.

As a child, she had a disconnect with reality, which made her lack any shred of empathy towards any creature she encountered. She would rip the wings off butterflies and take in pets that she would not feed. She had no feelings towards the living. Her father realized at a young age that there was something different about his daughter. Her cruelty was not malicious; it was just purely unfeeling. She never showed fear or remorse towards anything; she was a true sociopath.

He feared she would be unable to live in normal society, so at six years old, he gave her to the military to be a servant and receive firm discipline for her aversion. A Susian commander realized her disconnection soon after she arrived, and she was shown directly to the Immortals to be raised as their own.

This was a life of repeated rape and violence, but she liked the feeling of being forced to do things against her will, so she excelled in their presence. She was the only female to survive being thrown into their ranks. They respected her cruelty, and they reveled in her bloodlust. With her beauty masking her savagery, she was a spy of the highest order.

Aurias threw a bucket of freezing cold creek water onto her face; she instantly returned to reality, back into this violent world of give and take. The pain was excruciating; nothing in her training had prepared her for this ultra-sadistic interrogation. Ashkan questioned her once more, "How did you find us?!"

"I will tell you, please, I beg of you to stop this!" she said with an odd laugh.

Aurias pulled the horses back a step. The pressure released a bit.

The assassin gasped in relief, her voice wavering as she spoke now in perfect Greek, "King Xerxes sent me to find you scum!"

Aurias yelled back in Greek, "Why did you choose this place to search for us?"

There was no answer from the assassin as she faded back into a dream state.

The Immortals named her Azhi after the serpent. She would poison her victims with a venom-tipped dagger. The blade was gifted to her by Raza Douul himself. She would dip it in the refined juice of death cap mushrooms and let it dry repeatedly on the tip. Then, her unsuspecting prey would fall victim to a minor scrape on a crowded street, succumbing to its toxicity by the next meal.

Aurias again threw cold water onto the girl as she thrust awake. "Why did you choose this place to search for us!" he yelled. He pulled the dagger from its sheath and noticed the discoloration on the tip. He had heard of witches like this who would poison the strongest warrior without any fight or physical coercion. He teased the dagger tip on his fingertip and noticed her eyes following too eagerly.

The assassin replied, "We cast a broad net looking for you. I was told to cover this area to the north."

Panothos asked, "How many of you were sent to look for us?"

"There are only four of us, one for each corner of the empire," she cried out.

Panothos nodded to Aurias, and the horses took a small step forward. You could hear the ropes stretch and creak. The assassin screamed out in pain.

"How many of you are there?!" he screamed to her.

She lost consciousness again. Aurias tossed another bucket of cold creek water on her face, and she came to again, gasping desperately in pain.

"I told you, please! There are only four!"

Aurias and the horses took another small step forward. You could hear the assassin's joints pop and crackle as they stretched. She made the face of screaming out, but no noise escaped from her mouth, only the expression of intense pain and air. Panothos nodded, and Aurias moved the horses a step back again. Her body fell limp to the ground. She cried out, hyperventilating.

"Please, I beg of you, I tell you the truth."

Ashkan knelt and whispered to her in her native tongue, "Please tell them what they wish to hear; I cannot bear to watch anyone suffering like this."

She gasped to find the breath to speak ... "We are many; we are one ... we are not looking for you; you were never lost.

"We are everywhere in our lands and yours. You will never escape! Your little revolt will be put down, and you will be slaughtered like the unclean pigs that you are! The god-king Xerxes will not take any pity on you when you are captured. There is no place you will ever be safe; your fate has been sealed. Your heads will be mounted on sticks and taken to the corners of the kingdom for all the people to witness what happens when one crosses the kindness of our fair and noble king! You were born of whore cunts, and will die like worms, crushed into the ground under the hooves of our complete domination!"

Aurias pierced Azhi's skin with the tip of her tainted dagger, burying it into the vein on her neck and twisting it back and forth; she gasped in horrified disbelief; then, very slowly, foam began frothing from her mouth as her body started convulsing and contorting.

He stood tall, dropping the dagger next to her shaking body; he drew his sword then slapped the one of the horse's hind quarters with its flat side. The beast fearfully reared up and lunged forward. Azhi's joints began to tear, pop, and separate. No more words came from her mouth, only air and foaming, bloody saliva. Her eyes began to roll back in her head, blood leaking from her nose and mouth, and then, with a final wretched noise that sounded like hemp rope tearing, the horses pulled away, taking the upper portion of her arms and ripping them from her still-shuddering torso.

Ashkan recoiled, turning away quickly, and heaved his guts into the sand. He had never contemplated such a horrific scenario to ever play out before his eyes like this. He had never imagined he would ever bear witness to such a disturbing

125

incident. *Why have the gods been so unkind to bring me into this treacherous world, into the vast arena of unimaginable cruelty to which I am now so intimately betrothed?* His fate was now meshed with the sadistic impulses of these beastly soldiers. He balled up into the fetal position in the dirt and sobbed uncontrollably.

Aurias kicked dirt on him, grabbed him, and pulled him back up to his feet. He clutched Ashkan's forehead and forced open his eyes with his fingers so he could bear witness to what happened when you crossed them. "You see, boy? Do you see?

"What the insides of a beautiful devil look and smell like! Does she remind you of your goddamn mother, you wretched little worm?

"This is your fate if you do not do exactly what we tell you! I will personally ensure to deliver you to your maker ... in small pieces!" Then Aurias pushed the boy's head to the ground and walked away. Ashkan recoiled back into the fetal position, weeping.

The arduous march that followed was an actual test of endurance, escaping through the wilderness, paranoid of the pursuing Hydra nipping at their heels from any direction. For the moment, the group stayed on the southeastern side of the mountain range and followed the shoreline.

Panothos was nervous being pinched between the mountains and the inland sea. He knew the tactical disadvantage of using the path of least resistance. Still, his current "good" options were dwindling, especially now that he knew spies were everywhere in these lands, searching ruthlessly for them.

If they used the waterway, they risked contact with a well-fortified, armed bireme. Staying on the cart path, they risked being seen by locals or sentries ... Head for the mountain passes too early, and it would slow the exhausted procession down to barely a snail's crawl.

But what is the better option? Panothos wondered. *Expeditiously moving through loose rocks with constant elevation changes, rapidly changing mountain weather, and hazardous terrain?* With this path, one was always risking injury or finding dead-end trails that may have to be backtracked and rerouted around, sapping everyone's energy and leaving doubts about the quality of his leadership.

This time, against all practical wisdom, the best way was still the path of least resistance on the established cart trail. The group debated the plan and decided this made the most sense, moving faster during the night on obvious trails rather than in the daylight and possibly risking detection by more assassins.

According to Ashkan and the maps, only small fishing villages were on this route, but they would still go around them cautiously so they would not alert the locals. The girls were nominally skilled with the horses, so they would ride with the soldiers and sometimes walk alongside the stoic procession; some began to form close bonds with the Greek soldiers as they began learning one another's virtues.

Gyttja was now the girls' unspoken leader: a pale-skinned blonde woman with a muscular build. When she stood next to Panothos, she appeared to be slightly taller than he, so when she approached the Spartan leader, she would lower her head to appear shorter to him.

Panothos always noticed her humble nature and was taken by her unique attitude and beautiful features. She had made tremendous efforts over his time of internment to teach Panothos fragments of her native tongue. When Panothos was recovering from his wounds in Persepolis, Gyttja sat with him daily and unremittingly nursed him back to better health. A bond had formed between them; when they would rest in camp during the day, she would stay close to Panothos and give him the first pick of available food.

Panothos never imagined in his wildest dreams that the group would make it as far as they had, so deep inside enemy lands. He knew the odds were stacked against them; none of the soldiers imagined actually making it out of Persian territory alive; they just wanted a good death! Still, he reckoned it wasn't an entirely futile effort … it was better than the life of servitude that had almost become cemented in his future until these last few perilous weeks.

Panothos, in the recesses of his mind, still thought of his wife occasionally, but he knew she was as good as dead to him now; it was just the Spartan way for her to move on with her life. "Do or die" was this culture's philosophy, and it was a harsh, ingrained idealism.

Panothos felt the odds of them making it to the cold lands of the north were still very much against them. At this point, life expectancy was numbered in hours, not even days. The gods had already played a cruel trick on him, letting him survive such acute injuries at the hot gates; it was the fiercest fighting he had ever been a party to. All his brothers-in-arms had been slaughtered in the battle with his king, save the handful still by his side; they had also been fate's pawns.

He was now dead to his family and being hunted by a power-thirsty king who would expend great wealth to recapture his breathing trophies. Possibly, this compulsion was driven by not wanting to be seen as fallible. By this twisted logic,

Panothos contemplated what exactly their future might become.

Suicide was the undignified way of a coward. To die in battle was acceptable, but he could not meet a foe that could match or rise and kill him in a battle. The only option left was to fight, to battle to stay alive, and afterward try to live well enough to make the effort worth the steep price they would indeed have to pay.

They made camp far off the trail near some caves the scouts had stumbled upon earlier in the night. It would be incredibly warm, judging by the early morning temperatures. The caves would offer some reprieve from the scalding heat; it would be as good a time as any to rest and reset.

Panothos awoke in a sweat; he had dreamt of making love to his wife on their wedding night. He looked over at Gyttja as she still lay sleeping. Thoughts swirled endlessly in his head about the past and future. He did miss his wife immensely, but this was a futile mindset that must be shed; he reminded himself that what was done was done, and nothing would change the momentum or consequences of that fact.

He pulled the animal skins over Gyttja's bare shoulders; she moved in closer, nestling into him invitingly. This excited Panothos; he had not felt these feelings in a very long time. It made him feel the same passion as when he was a young man.

Panothos' parents had chosen him to be coupled in an arranged marriage with a young girl, the beautiful Isadora. He never imagined that she would not be a part of his future. He had noticed her from the time she was only twelve years of age. He had a crush on her as a young man; as it happens, she was the daughter of one of Panothos' father's most trusted friends, Menares. Both families were secure in their wealth, so they decided to couple their children as was the custom of the time. When Isadora was fifteen, she was betrothed to Panothos and expected to bring a healthy male heir to their families. The gods, as frivolous as they seemed at times, did not grant the couple this simple wish. The first child died at birth.

The next child also died a few days after its birth, which depressed young Isadora for some time. After the miscarriage and the second child's passing, she was never quite the same; she blamed herself for infertility, but honestly, there was no way to tell the valid reason for it. The two tried to conceive an heir for Panothos, but it never came to be. Panothos promised to love Isadora whether or not they could have children, but this was a mere consolation to her. When Panothos left for the hot gates, Isadora was stoic; she was somewhat glad she could think about something other than her lack of birthing an heir for at least a short while.

Gyttja rolled over and opened her haunting blue eyes. The first thing she saw was Panothos staring directly at her. She smiled, and Panothos instinctually leaned in close to kiss her. She did not pull away from him. He had a gentle touch and a kind demeanor for such a battle-hardened warrior. Time stopped in its tracks, and the world around disappeared. The two began passionately probing each other with their lips. For Gyttja, this was the first time she had not been forcibly made to be intimate, and she had never felt this way before.

When Gyttja was a young girl, she was picking berries in the woods for her uncle when Utlagr horsemen approached, creeping up on her and some of the girls from the village, forcing them into chains and then thrusting them into a life of slavery. She was then traded into Persian captivity by raiders from the steppes who sold her when she was a mere eleven years of age.

Physical abuse and hard labor were all she endured for three more long years while they kept her at one of the kingdom's northernmost outposts. At fourteen, she was taken to the palace in Persepolis. She was somewhat underdeveloped and homely, still viewed almost as a child by the other servant girls, who kept her away from the wicked glances of the Persian commanders for as long as they could.

A year later, once permanently housed inside the palace, the older Arab servant girls, jealous of her easy life, fixed her looks and dressed her in Persian attire; this showed off her now rapidly developing body. They adorned her in scented oils and ornate polished stones. At first, she loved to be made up this way, feeling the attention was a good thing. She enjoyed the adulation, but when they made her look more adult and beautiful, the physical abuse instantly changed to a more sinister abuse and overt sexual exploitation.

When a prince or a lower caste of royalty came to the palace to stay, she would be given to the men to do with her as they pleased. She tried to resist, but the price of resistance was sometimes extremely high; beatings and rape were common amongst the girls who resisted, so rather than take a beating, she would comply and try to hurry through the ugly event using her sensuality to speed up the encounter.

However, Panothos was the first man she had ever met in her entire life who treated her honorably and demanded nothing from her in return; she was genuinely grateful to him.

Panothos wrapped his strong hands around the small of her back and pulled her close to him. He felt the heat from her body burning against his; her pulse quickened as he pulled her in closer. He could feel her heart beating rhythmically in a rough syncopation with his. This was the first moment in as long as they could remember that they had felt genuinely human again.

He noticed her milky white skin contrasting with his scarred flesh and olive-tanned body; it excited him. He kissed her lips, staring intensely into her eyes as they witnessed each other's soul. He gently caressed her neck, tasting her essence and the salt of her sweat. They massaged each other's bodies, delighting in every contour and texture as they endlessly explored. He was kissing her chest, caressing her breasts, exploring, licking, and teasing. Slowly and lovingly, he wanted to learn every square millimeter of her body.

She shuddered in delight at every advance that he made. She was totally saturated, ready, and welcoming of his advances. Spreading open her legs to let him enter, she slowly guided him inside her, and the two became one creature, bonded by fate, pulsating in a temporary reprieve from the harsh world that plagued them. However, this hardship had still ultimately brought them together in this moment as unassuming lovers. Her skin quivered uncontrollably as he touched her; she had never experienced such intense feelings. Never had intercourse been so gentle and never before so intense and enjoyable.

Panothos, having been married to an emotionally delicate woman, knew exactly how to touch her; Gyttja smiled at him with a pleasurably guilty grin. In the past weeks, he had pondered how she might react, and he was pleasantly surprised that she reciprocated his desire entirely and without reservations. He knew at any point since the moment he awoke in the palace, he could have had his way with her or any of the others, but without the chase, the moment would have lacked any shred of decency and real meaning.

Finally, just as she began climaxing, with one last thrust, he spent his seed in a long-needed release … He pulled her in tightly, as close as two humans could be. She lay undulating, erotically impaled, pulsating in pleasure beneath the fortress of his constricting mass. Indeed, living at this moment was so much better than conceding their autonomy back at the palace. They both needed this release, and Panothos had secretly longed for it since feeling Gyttja's touch for the first time. The stress of the past few seasons temporarily melted away as their sweat combined and lubricated their bodies. They stared deep into each other's souls for a brief moment of mutual elation, locked together in passion, not wanting it ever to end.

Panothos had not felt this kind of unrestrained ecstasy with Isadora in a very long time. He knew in his bones that he would never see her again. Maybe the gods would be displeased with him forsaking his marital vows, but they had forsaken him entirely by not letting him die on the battlefield, so fuck the gods, he vowed to himself. They were again absent, just as anticipated, and when their blessing was most needed, they had given him a cruel twist of fate that burned like a venomous snakebite.

After some time, he kissed Gyttja on her glistening breasts, then neck, then lips. He slowly raised and stretched, kissing her forehead as he rose, and then he walked over to the entrance of the cave, cooling his bare body in its consistent outward breeze. At least for this brief moment in time … today was turning out to be an excellent day to be still among the living.

Chapter 6

The Long Way Out

Panothos and the others, after an actual full day's rest, marched on, approaching the corridor to ascend the Caucasus. Today, they would move in the daylight to see what this terrain had in store. Panothos was weary of traversing the available route around this mountain pass, but there were few realistic options to go in this direction; the other route pinched him much too tightly to the water, exposing them to multiple angles of attack. As they pushed up the narrow, steep trail, they passed carcasses of abandoned wagons and beasts of burden, which had succumbed to the volatility of the hostile terrain.

Several days had passed since they executed the beautiful assassin on the bank of the small creek. Now, her handlers probably knew which direction to search and which path they would be obligated to choose. They would know this simply from her not checking in with them and from their firsthand knowledge of their domain.

Panothos' senses spiked on high alert again as the caravan inched slowly forward in the parched mountain air. He positioned scouts at intervals ahead so they could relay any tactical information back to the group's main body before problems were directly upon them. So far, none had returned with any critical news, nor had they built signal fires to warn of approaching enemy fighters. Panothos would soon be reaching the end of the territorial map he had gained from the raid on the training encampment outside of Persepolis on the first night of escape. He was losing his modest advantage due to the unknown variables ahead. From here forth, they were making their future one hard-earned step at a time.

Ashkan looked on in amazement across the vista at the rugged beauty at the edge of the mapped Persian lands. The peaks were snow-covered; vegetation stopped at these higher elevations on the mountains and gave way to rocks and small scrub brush and lichen. He had never ventured so far to the outer edge of the empire, and now he, too, was in uncharted territory. His father, once a trader, told him stories of far-off places, tribes, and whole countries conquered by Cyrus the Great. Now, oddly enough, as a prisoner, he was seeing first-hand the farthest reaches of the greater Persian Empire.

They slowly progressed up the treacherous mountain passes he had heard of as a child, in what he had previously imagined were mythical legends and the grandiose tall tales of aging old men, but here they were, right in front of his face, all true.

The group kept advancing until even breathing became a labored action. Many of the Greeks were becoming dizzy and sick, thus slowing the already creeping advance. Even the three Spartans, who had trained to combat this adversity, found it challenging to proceed. The higher up the mountain they climbed, the thinner and colder the air became. They pushed hard to move fast up the trail, but they were losing daylight, and the temperature began to plummet as the peak's shadow overtook their position.

The men shivered and huddled close to their steeds, and the girls pulled their bodies in tightly with the soldiers. They found no caves on this route, but the moon was more than half full in the sky and still partially illuminated the pathway, so it wasn't impossible to pass through without torches. Panothos' mostly healed injuries ached in the extreme cold temperatures they were encountering; every step was simply excruciating.

They dismounted their horses and walked beside them on the inside wall, trying to hide from the blowing winds and keep their bodies warm by the shelter of the animals. Some of their horses had given up entirely in the middle of the night and lay dead with exhaustion. The men slaughtered them and bundled some of the meat inside their own hides before it eventually froze to a solid.

The procession had slowed to barely a crawl, so for hours, the group crept forward, stopping to rest often at places that offered some cover. Panothos ordered them to make a quick camp because the temperature was so miserably cold. "Circle the horses around the perimeter; tie them together so they don't wander. They will shield us from some of this wind!

"Everyone needs to group together tightly, share the warmth, and try to nap until morning light breaks!" he ordered.

The exhausted group had no more energy left and were reasonably confident they could overtake the summit during daylight hours once it was warmer. The cold temperatures would not allow them to proceed, making every move absolutely unbearable, so biding their time seemed the best solution. They clustered together and draped themselves in every piece of hide or cloth they possessed, though it just barely helped to shield them from the cold. The air was crisp, and they were so close to the stars and moon that it almost seemed as if you could reach out and touch them. Such beauty to behold, but with so much agony to endure.

It was a long night; minutes seemed like hours in the numbing cold; on and on, the suffering continued relentlessly. After what seemed like an eternity, they awoke, and the sun's first rays finally peeked out from behind the frigid dark horizon. Steam rose off the horses' fur as they began to warm.

They found one of the Greek men, Aias, had frozen to death where he lay in the outer perimeter of the huddle; he did so silently, and none around him realized it until they stirred. Another of the horses fell victim to nature's calm fury, collapsed, and froze as they slept. The extreme temperatures had levied a steep toll on the men this dark and bitter night.

Stiffly arising in the early light, they stood in the sun's rays until their toes and hands began to itch from the feeling returning. They knew that the ascent would be challenging, and it was just as they had come to imagine. They stacked stones onto Aias' body, said a few words of remembrance, then broke camp and pressed forward towards the summit.

It took most of the day and early evening to reach the mountain's summit, but at least the sun's rays warmed them for the most grueling parts of the crossing. They were cold, weak, and exhausted, but Panothos would not let them build fires to keep warm; still so high on the mountain's face, it was almost impossible to get wood to burn anyway. It would have mostly smoldered in the thin air; he knew such a fire would be seen for many stades, so he thought it better to air on the side of caution.

The group traversed the summit in the afternoon, finally conquering the rugged ascent, and began descending rapidly down the other side on a much broader path. They were making good time on their way to a thickly forested plateau they could vaguely see below; they would camp and rest before the dark of night fell.

Just then, the forward scout Aristos approached; he had been sent out earlier to survey the options before them and returned hastily to report what he had witnessed much further down the trail. He sprinted up to Panothos, trying to catch his breath and brief him.

"Sir, we spotted a sizeable expeditionary force of what looks to be 400 or more soldiers digging in at the base of the trailhead."

He took another moment to try and slow his breathing before speaking again. "There was a small group of heavy cavalry, a large group of infantry soldiers, and one group of what looked to be 'Immortals,' but I couldn't get close enough to confirm this. They have split their forces into three fronts, one group fortifying an ambush at the bottom of the trail; the others are posted up in the camp, another guarding their rear in reserve!"

"Thank you, Aristos, you have done well," Panothos replied.

Aristos sat down, still breathing heavily. Sigrun approached and shared some of her water with him; he thanked her after regaining his composure and rose back to his feet, awaiting further orders.

They wanted to descend from the mountain pass undetected. But now they were trapped atop the trail by the Persian force.

"There are two routes with a few options, sir, but neither looks to be great ... nor do we think we could make it undetected."

"The first option is to backtrack a bit and climb the next peak over with no trail and then traverse to the southwest in the opposite direction we wish to advance.

"The second option is to go north in the direction of the Persian line. But there is a caveat: there is a twenty-meter cliff that we could descend and do so in the middle of the night. If we did it undetected, we could raid the camp from its back corner; only then, might we have a fighting chance to make it off this damned rock!" Aristos exclaimed.

Trying to advance headfirst into an ambush would be a suicide mission, Panothos understood immediately, so it was off the table for discussion. Doubling back towards Persepolis over an even higher section of the mountain range by foot seemed an exercise in exhausting futility; the freezing temperatures alone would probably kill most of the group, and the whole endeavor would end entirely in vain, with only a few survivors, making all the previous struggle totally for naught. The only logical step was the most complex option: to descend the cliff face and attack the enemy camp as Aristos recommended. Aurias, listening closely, approached Panothos and told him his thoughts.

"I can lead a team of twelve men down the cliff in the middle of the night and regroup silently on the backside of the enemy tents. We will wait to attack until just before dawn's light breaks."

Panothos nodded in approval. Aurias continued, "Tyranos and the other three men will descend the trail to the edge of the tree line in the middle of the night, right before dawn, and ignite a large brush fire on the main path; hopefully, this will entice a portion of the Persian force to investigate the fire. Once I see the glow and smoke plume from the fire, I will infiltrate and execute a raid on the camp from inside its boundaries. When we have slain the sentries, we will ignite anything flammable in the camp and try to create a real firestorm of confusion. They will not know where our forces are attacking from.

"Then, once the Persian force is split into two fronts, my men will form an ambush at the cliff face behind the camp where they descended the wall. Panothos, you and the rest of the group will hurl down large stones and arrows, and rain silent death upon them from the cliff face. The Persians sent to attack us at the base of the cliff will think that we are all they are fighting, not knowing yet of the team lurking above us out of their sight line. You will use the weight of the thrown stones to make our earthen missile more volatile, just like before in the training camp!

"This will leave you out of reach of their archers and leave me to hook around on both sides and counterattack while the Persians' attention is focused up on the cliff. They will not know exactly where to counter, with the scourge of spears, stones, and arrows damning their every movement. They will be illuminated from our primary incursion and should be easy targets."

Panothos figured Aurias' plan was the most realistic way to achieve victory. This was the best option for such a small group of fighters to have a real chance at survival. If all the Persian troops focused their attack with full force in one area or the other, the plan would fall apart quickly and miserably, and they would all spill their blood in battle, which he reasoned was also an acceptable outcome but not as welcoming!

Gyttja approached Panothos and asked, "May I speak with you, please?" He nodded and gave her his full attention. "I have spoken with the other girls, and we want you to know that we would rather die fighting in combat than be taken prisoner by these swine! We will gladly bear arms to defend ourselves and be useful if you let us. We have often watched you train and wish to be of service."

Panothos smiled at her; he was utterly smitten with her bravery.

"Come with me, Gyttja. Your strength gives us strength; you all will definitely hold the line with us, our warrior maidens!"

He gathered the women and gave them the bows and arrows they still possessed, and shields and daggers in case the enemy got in close. Gyttja smiled proudly. Panothos showed them the proper stance and ensured they all had the strength to pull back on the bowstring and raise the shields. They were, after all, servants in the palace; they were strong from the burdens of their slavery and were not afraid of these Persian men. He quickly explained the plan to them, and they soon learned the fundamentals of combat.

For the next couple of hours, the men raced under the cover of darkness into their attack positions, sneaking a couple of moments of rest before the melee was to begin. Aurias and his team descended the cliff face in the dark, sliding down improvised ropes; they hurried into their positions. Aristos, Aurias, and a few of the Greeks who came down the cliff face made a small incursion into the outermost sentry post and eliminated a few guards, silently slicing their throats and hiding their bodies.

They took some of the dead men's uniforms, put them on over the top of their clothing, and replaced the sentries with their own disguised men. They then daringly took a walk into the camp to see the strength of the force. Aristos and Aurias could walk freely around inside the camp in these uniforms. They quickly identified the weak points and mapped out the strongest fortifications.

They stumbled upon an armory tent with more strange black bottles like the ones they had seen at Thermopylae. The Persian shock troops would stuff a piece of fabric into the neck of a bottle, light it on fire, and hurl it towards the center of the phalanx. When it landed, it would shatter and explode. The explosion would spread the liquid fire and shards of pottery everywhere within its radius, igniting everything it touched, including flesh, turning everything around into a blazing inferno. They stole only a few of these dark bottles from deep inside the crates so the theft would not be readily apparent.

They cut a sizeable gaping slit in the top of the tent where the incendiary devices were being stored. Aurius left Ciaphus, a young Athenian, behind the armory dressed in a Persian sentry's uniform; he waited to hurl one of the lit bottles into the armory tent once the attack was underway.

The remaining men from the raiding party retreated to the cliff face's base and prepared for the attack to commence. They roped up several black bottles, and Panothos disbursed them accordingly. The other men hid behind boulders in the perimeter, waiting like hunters in the shadows, ready to pounce on their prey. The men knew they were vastly outnumbered and would be fighting for their very existence at the mountain's base, so coordinating the assault was crucial.

Tyranos and his small team made their way down the mountain trail to the tree line, gathering tinder in the darkness, waiting patiently for the pre-dawn light to graze the stratosphere so that they could set the forest ablaze.

Gyttja and the palace girls, with the help of the remaining hoplites, finished gathering perfectly sized stones and stacked piles of them on the cliff's edge, ready to be heaved down upon the Persian counterattack.

Just as the sun violated the darkness, gently painting the sky in a warming hue, a second glow illuminated the mountain face just below the tree line.

Tyranos and his men, just upwind of the evergreen forest near where the tree line began to thicken, ignited piles of pine needles with one of the torches, and the parched, resinous tinder piles went up in flames so rapidly the men barely escaped the spread of the blaze on the uphill side. They then fired flaming arrows down the mountain pass into mounds of dead evergreen bows and kindling they had built up in the night on the lower plateaus below, where the Persian advance would have no choice but to ascend the trail.

The Greeks knew this was the sign to begin their counterassault! As the Persians marched up the trail to punish the escapees, they found themselves pinched between the two fires, with one side unpassable due to the size of the existing flames and the extreme heat of the large trees that were fully engulfed. On the other side, the two fires from the arrows raced up towards them, crossing the trail and cutting them off from retreating down the path. The men panicked and ran in both directions, trying to make their way to safety through what seemed to be voids in the inferno.

Tyranos' group met those who came up the mountain path through an ashy gap just off the trail's side. Their vision was blurry from the extreme heat and unavoidable smoke. Tyranos and his men cut them down one by one as they exited the fiery gauntlet. The many who retreated down the trail perished in the new raging inferno that was being pushed by the wind directly back on their position. One could see men's hair combusting as they fell, screams of agonizing death mixing with the rumble of the blaze that echoed throughout the canyon walls.

Most of the oxygen was sucked into the flames, and the men who were not being engulfed by them just started falling on their knees to the ground inside the growing firestorm as they gasped for the last breaths of air. Like micro tornadoes, vortexes spun into the air, igniting the new tinder, pulling in all the oxygen that was left, and combusting everything in their path.

Ciaphus, left behind at the enemy tent, saw the glow; he lit and hurled the flaming, explosive-filled container into the cut opening of the armory tent where the rest of the bottles were stored. He hurried back towards the cliff face, crouching, waiting for an explosion. Then, just as the first rays of light pierced the dawn, chaos unleashed itself in all its magnitude. Audacity would reign supreme on this battlefield, on this tiny patch of burning ground secluded from a vast, unknowing world.

A colossal explosion detonated in the armory tent and sent a fireball mushrooming thirty or more meters into the air, sending shards of flaming pottery and burning tent stakes down onto the encampment. Ciaphus, unaware of how large the explosion would be, was forced to take shelter from the fiery rain to keep from becoming a casualty of his own volley.

The girls on the cliff's top could feel the fireball's warmth! Persian soldiers ran in all directions, trying to figure out where the commotion originated and where their units were. A column of Persian soldiers at the base of the pass raced up the main trail to try and join up with their forces, who had gone ahead through the forest blaze that was now sweeping across the mountain pass. They knew it had to be the Spartans who had started the blaze, and a sickening fear began to drench their spirits when none of the first waves of soldiers from the assault were standing behind the line of flames. They only saw fetal-shaped lumps of char the size of bodies amongst the burning underbrush and pines.

Another Persian unit was returning to the camp to receive their next assignment just as Aurias and his men began to light the other tents in the back of the camp on fire. Aristos and his men began advancing on the approaching Persian reserve troops dressed in Persian sentry uniforms; they attacked the unit in a full-frontal assault, thus drawing the disorganized soldiers into counterattacking without grouping into a formal battle formation, drawing them out chaotically into the breach.

Aurias and the remainder of his men began their assault on the Persian flank as soon as this last cluster of reserve troops had passed by them.

His men swept around and charged their rear, pressing the Persian force between his two small groups, simultaneously pushing them nearer the cliff face. As the cascading explosions from the armory and the fast-moving fire in the forest persisted, Aristos and his men withdrew back to the rock wall.

The Persians broke rank in confusion and tried to advance on them to finish the Greek troops off. Aurias and his team on one flank made a hasty retreat to the far side of the cliff face, giving the Persians room to group up into columns. The Persians began to march in step to the cliff wall, forming tight formations to trap and finish them off.

Split into two groups, the Greeks had their backs up against the cliff wall and were set to repel the coming wave. The Persians halted their advance and started deploying their archers in columns. Aurias and his men raised their shields above their heads and took cover from the arrows; as they crouched behind the cover, they began to hear loud thuds and the sound of men screaming. Panothos and the girls on the top of the cliff were hurling stones and arrows at the archers.

Panothos then lit the last black bottles and flung them long at the advancing Persian infantry. They landed behind the archers' formations, hitting the middle of the infantry column, now perfectly silhouetted by the many fires blazing unchecked behind them. The men began collapsing as the stones and arrows rained down on them, many more scurrying away on fire from the flames that had spread from the shattered bottles. The stones, almost like magic, instantly appeared out of the darkness of the cliff's shadow, seen only by their targets seconds before impact.

Because the archers had drawn their bows and draped their shields over their backs, they had nothing to protect their heads with as the stones and arrows began raining silently from the pale abyss of the early morning sky. Aurias and his team then ran around the Persian formation and attacked on their left with contempt, as the Persians were now fixated on the attack from above. The three-pronged attack began decimating the off-balance Persian columns.

Once the cliff face was secure, Aurias and his men began disrobing the fallen Persians and camouflaging themselves in more of the dead soldiers' uniforms. The chaos had gotten so completely out of hand that the Persian officers were losing control of their formations within the confines of their own makeshift encampment.

Sensing imminent collapse, the Persian forward commander yelled to the scattering troops to re-form their broken formations near the trail base. As the soldiers assembled, Aurias and his men assimilated into their ranks and joined at the rear of one of the columns. They marched double time to the base of the mountain pass to fortify the Persian troops behind the fire line and finish the job.

Tyranos and Panothos rallied on the mountainside, penetrating through a gap in the blaze where all the pine needles and branches had burned away to gray ashes and tiny embers. They had the high ground but were still vastly outnumbered. As the columns of Persian soldiers advanced up the pass to meet them, they counterattacked with Gyttja and the others; their faces were smudged in charcoal. They fired their arrows first over the heads of Panothos' line, and then when they were out of arrows, they started throwing homemade wooden spears they had carved and accumulated along the journey.

The rear of the Persian attack had devolved into complete confusion in the early morning light. The Persian captain, realizing the dysfunction in the state of his troops, was completely overtaken with a dreadful panic. He was about to be overrun and so decided to release his Immortal shock troops to counterattack the Greek advance up the base of the mountain trail.

The group with the camouflaged Greeks approached the rear of the marching column; Aurias and his men began to stab and quickly take out the Persian regulars from behind one at a time until they finally reached the column of Immortals.

The Immortals' advance was so focused on retaking the front line that they didn't even notice they were being picked off piecemeal from behind. Now, far in the rear of his troops, the commander could see the ineffectiveness of the advances and looked on in panicked disbelief; this couldn't be happening. He quietly told his staff to prepare an exit.

As they neared the skirmish line, Aurias could make out the looming backlit silhouette of his fellow Greeks on the high ground. His team broke rank and, all at once, began hacking at the middle of the formation, causing them to split and turn around to fight the new menace within their own ranks. Panothos saw the line split and pivot; he knew his men were responsible for this and rallied a charge down the trail and into the middle of the fray, further splitting the Persian advance.

The overly panicked Persian commander had entirely underestimated what a small group of desperate, well-trained soldiers could do to his massive force. After only a few minutes, Tyranos and Aurias finally fought their way up to each other at the phase line and made eye contact, now completely severing the Persian line. A few Greek soldiers had fallen but were again ruling the battlefield. Tyranos had taken a good slice on his leg, but it did not hinder his effectiveness; he fought on like a monster!

The Immortals were missing an essential weapon from their arsenal: the explosive bottles ... Once that veil of trickery was removed from the equation, they fought like any other soldiers.

The camp was smoldering; the Persian troops on the hill didn't know which way to go because they were being murdered from every direction they tried to advance. With his private guard, the commander began sensing this dysfunction and, in utter desperation, decided to save his wealthy skin and escape without calling general retreat for the remainder of his troops. They dropped everything and ran, leaving the remaining Persian troops to die at the hands and blades of the battle-hardened, blood-lusting Greek warriors.

The dawn's faint glow had expired, and the morning sun showed its full radiance. The carnage, once obscured by the darkness, became fully apparent. When the Persian regulars saw their commander and his private cohort guard retreating without warning behind them, they threw down their weapons and chased behind, simply running for their lives. The Immortals, as focused and disciplined as they were, continued to fight furiously until their last man fell, never looking back at their retreating commander. They would fight until they were finished, bloody, and bludgeoned; these men fought hard and died honorable deaths.

Billowing gray smoke rose from the burning forest, horses ran free, and the bodies of wounded soldiers scattered all over the battlefield came clearly into crisp focus in the glaring light of morning. Panothos and his men triumphed with simple tactics and the unswerving desire to survive. They beat all of the odds that were stacked so ominously against them. Three more of the Greek warriors, Aetos, Damianos, and Xanthe, had fallen in the battle, and a Persian arrow had mortally wounded poor young Aesa; she would not remain much longer in this cruel and indifferent world. Gyttja, Sigrun, and the other girls gathered to help her cross into the afterlife with her spirit intact.

Aesa, with tears streaming, tried to hold on, asking for her mother repeatedly as the spark of life faded from her open eyes. She was so young, and she had never even known the love of a man. Gyttja, quietly sobbing, rocked and cradled her as she slipped into oblivion, finally lowering the girl's head to the ground as tears rolled down her reddened cheeks, wetting Aesa's face and the dirt she lay on. She gently closed Aesa's eyelids one last time with her fingertips. As tough as Gyttja was, so much loss exacted a heavy toll on her emotionally. It calloused her, tempering her resolve to find a way home.

Panothos and his men descended the rest of the way down the mountain pass to the flats below;

they had no time to mourn the fallen. To stop the Persian commander from escaping, Aurias and five of his warriors on horseback gave chase, killing the retreating soldiers as they gained on them. Sooner or later, these men would try once more to take their lives, so now was the right time to slaughter this enemy in retreat.

They galloped up to the water's edge just as the bireme was pulling away from the shallows with its sails up, pushing it rapidly out to the depths. They would have to miss the opportunity to take this commander's head today. The Persian commander had yet to learn how few men had toppled his ambush with his back turned in shameless retreat.

Still, though Aurias missed his escaping prey, he figured Xerxes would surely finish the job for such drastic insubordination after such a lopsided victory. With Panothos' numbers slowly dwindling, he knew they would not be so lucky to achieve another one-sided victory such as this; it was just impossible with so few men and now more injured. Thus far, they had only been lucky not to meet a well-organized force.

As Aurias and the Greeks returned to the enemy camp, they murdered the rest of the wounded Persians where they lay. The girls quickly gathered all the provisions they could carry for the next leg of the journey as the mercy killings continued. The Persians had abandoned all their battle wagons during their retreat, leaving the resources to be plundered. The fire on the mountainside now burned out of control; billowing grayish-black smoke belched and crackled high into the sky.

At this point, Panothos contemplated; the best thing to do was get as far away from this smoke plume as possible. He needed to move as fast as he could and get the group underway, for it pinpointed their exact location, just in case any other units were sent to apprehend them or were camped nearby.

They cut away the sails of scuttled Persian troop boats and draped the battle wagons with them. They gathered at the water's edge to clean the blood and soot from their bodies and try to find a way to vacate the area more rapidly. Panothos did not want to risk getting attacked again because, right at this moment, they could not repel another assault in this condition. They were all far beyond exhausted; they needed rest, but even after such a lopsided victory, they would not be afforded such a luxury.

Ashkan looked on in amazement throughout the course of the battle at his captors' tactical prowess; he could see their knowledge of warfare unwaveringly on display. He knew in his heart that these men were some of the fiercest professional warriors ever to step foot on a battlefield. They dominated the simple Persian troops every time contact was made.

Exiting the enemy camp, they found a large wooden chest left behind, with its corner half buried in fresh mud; it must have been dropped from a wagon in the Persian commander's frightened rush to flee. When they pried open the trunk, on the lid, Ashkan could read the name of its owner, the commander who had fled the field of battle in fear for his life; Javid Hamedani, the provincial governor of Parthia.

Ashkan was shocked that such a powerful man had been dispatched to quell this escape. Two such influential Persian officers who touted battlefield supremacy in the public eye had now been clearly and bitterly routed by Panothos and his small, ragged band of soldiers and servant girls. Ashkan felt at this point that the gods must ultimately be on the side of the Greeks concerning matters of war.

Inside the abandoned trunk, Panothos found a large chain mail bag heavily laden and clad in the finest jewels. He surmised that it must be the governor's war chest. As a direct emissary of Xerxes, Governor Hamedani was permitted to raise an army of conscripts independently without Xerxes' oversight. To procure these forces, the Persians would pay tribute to the elder or chieftain of the empire's outlying villages, recruiting conscripts from the ranks of the local population.

He opened the bag, and a smile came to his face. Gyttja looked on in amazement at what she saw; the bag gleamed, containing more gold coins and gems than she had ever seen up close, even in the palace, where rich guests flaunted their immense wealth for sport.

Panothos reached in and showed Aurias large, raw golden nuggets, coins of many different conquered lands, and an array of jewels ... enough to buy favor in any kingdom. This changed everything; the nature of Panothos' strategy could now afford better tools and also afford them allies. This discovery may have just saved them from imminent annihilation.

Five days passed after the crushing defeat, and Governor Hamedani finally returned to Parthia, where Samid Al Sahan was waiting to receive his prisoners and return them to Persepolis. When Hamedani arrived with only his guard, no men, no captives, and no war chest, Samid went utterly berserk. He flung shields, swords, and plates at Governor Hamedani; although Hamedani outranked him, Samid's temper dispelled any notion of his lower rank in the Persian hierarchy.

Hamedani had been warned of the Spartan prowess in battle by Samid, but Hamedani had underestimated or didn't believe the stories of Panothos' warrior's tenacity. Samid was so insanely infuriated with the unsavory news that he ran his sword straight through two of the governor's returning personal guards in this violent outburst, slaughtering them where they stood.

He screamed at Hamedani, "If you were not so close to the royal family, I would execute you for dereliction of duty right here on the spot!" Samid was now entirely beside himself with pure rage, after two routing defeats, no less occurring on Persian home soil … It was absolutely unheard of.

Xerxes would not stand for this failure without taking the head of the one or all who had failed him so miserably. So, without dispatching a messenger to Persepolis to inform Xerxes of this foul news, Samid ordered Raza Douul to gather 1,000 reserve troops and able-bodied landowners from Parthia; he and Governor Hamedani would set out northward to finish off these Spartan miscreants on Samid's terms once and for all.

Chapter 7

"I am Your Sword!"

Panothos and his men pushed the carts and horses hard. They were utterly exhausted but knew that they had to keep moving. They were still alive and had a fighting chance to disappear forever into the vast wilderness of the uncharted northern lands. He decided against stopping to rest until they were well clear of the vast plume of smoke ever rising at his back, choosing to keep pushing north, trying to outrun the menace that seemed to overshadow them like some revealing specter.

Panothos calculated a roughly one-week lead in front of whatever retaliation Hamedani could mount against them. So, rather than stopping their progress, he let a portion of his crew sleep inside the newly acquired battle wagons, moving along the trail while the rest of the group drove them to new lands outside the greater Persian Empire. For days, the Spartans alternated shifts; Gyttja and the girls cared for the weak and wounded while in this state of endless motion.

The terrain was beginning to shift from a dry mountainous country into lush rolling hills and endless grassland prairies. They were now well outside of the known borders of the empire and were beginning to make their way onto the steps of the lower northern territories and into the uncharted.

Gyttja, now with a war horse of her own, gained from the camp, was growing into a leader, telling the others the plans and ensuring everyone in the group was cared for appropriately.

After a few days of strenuous progress, she approached ... "Panothos, I plead with you; we need to rest. We have been so many days in the harsh conditions of the mountains; we fought battles, lost friends, we go and go without rest, and need time for our bodies and minds to recover properly."

At first, Panothos was not receptive to the idea, but he, too, was exhausted and needed some time to reset. His muscles burned, and bones ached ... Only rest would help heal this pain.

"Yes, Gyttja, we need to do so. We also need to get as far away from this trouble as possible. You know that the Persians' pride has now been sullied; they will not let us escape without more blood spilled. I tell you this: I do not want to lose another because I choose to rest and not make enough distance between us and them!"

She grimaced and sighed. "I understand; I could not bear to lose another either. I have grown to feel that we are almost a family, bonded by our fate." Panothos nodded approvingly, conceding to her wisdom.

He halted the worn-down procession, telling them to make camp and rest up for the next leg of the journey.

Panothos and Gyttja rode out together ahead of the party and scouted the perimeter to verify that no dangers lurked nearby. They approached a very small village nestled in a shallow valley. The settlement looked to be nearly abandoned, and they cautiously dismounted their steeds and approached the village on foot.

The place was primarily home to old women and young children. Neither Gyttja nor Panothos recognized the villagers' words, but they could see fear and paranoia on their faces as the two strangers approached them. They were escorted to a roundhouse at the village's center, the village elder's home. They offered a few pieces of gold from the Persian war chest.

Gyttja could piece together a few words she had learned from some of the other slave girls back in the palace in Persepolis, and modestly communicated with the elder. He could understand enough of her words, and they could understand one another using hand gestures and drawing glyphs with a stick in the dirt. The elder told Gyttja the story of repeated Persian raids that ultimately killed or removed all the able-bodied warriors and older boys from the now almost-extinct village.

There were drawings of the battle scratched on the stone walls in a cellar where the villagers would seek shelter from the Persian marauders. The young men who weren't killed defending their families in the raids were conscripted into the Persian ranks or forced into slave labor. There, they died in the quarries from overwork and starvation from the diet of only lean rabbit meat given once a day if they were lucky.

The elder spoke of a great inland sea fed by a mighty river; there was a village on its banks where they might be able to offer shelter and safe passage. The villagers they spoke of were friendly to anyone but Persians and tried to resist them with their best efforts in past conflicts. The local fishermen of the village knew these waters and had ventured deep into them and then far up into the river inlet. He pointed to the northeast in the direction where they had just come from.

Panothos understood the elder's pointing and the dirt sketches. He understood that they might have to double back to the south, the way they had just been, and then turn to the north, which increased the risk of running headlong into the next wave of Persians that would most surely be tracking their progress by now.

They had become a tattered group, shrinking in numbers, and were now entirely exhausted. They needed an ally and much more than simple luck to make it through another battle. They didn't have the stamina for a conventional shield-to-shield confrontation. By now, the Persians must know they would try to avoid another one-on-one encounter and try covertly to survive with trickery and deception.

Again, Panothos needed to take a calculated risk that contradicted simple logic. He needed to step up into this new role as a leader of a tribe of men and women, dependent every day on his judgment to keep them alive and trying desperately to bring them all safely to their destination.

This almost impossible decision could lead to their downfall in one fell swoop, but the unexpected change of direction that the elder advised still gave them the best odds of survival of any route they might have taken before the meeting. Panothos had not seen any future since awakening in such a broken state after his capture, recuperating at the palace. But now, a future distinctly showed itself directly in front of them, and it was closer to becoming a reality than just the fever dream of a handful of forsaken, ragged ghosts.

Panothos and Gyttja returned to the encampment where Tyranos and Aurias had organized a perimeter night watch. Tyranos and Aurias had also erected makeshift quarters for the first night of slumber. Finally, inside and away from the elements after so many challenging days, they could now rest.

Panothos was given the main tent with furs and a straw mat on which to lay; he was their undisputed leader, and they treated him as such. He wanted no praise, nor did he feel he deserved the lavish cot they had prepared for him, initially offering it back to Aurias, but to no avail. They wanted him in charge, and without a vote or a word spoken, they made it clear that he was their chosen leader. He accepted this fate and thanked the men for their troubles, granting him these very comfortable, plush accommodations.

The bedding would allow his body to rest and heal; he had not been taking good care of himself on the trail, and his men needed him to recover. He looked at Gyttja and motioned for her to come inside with him. He had grown very fond of her and wished her permanently by his side whenever they had time to rest. They lay in the plush furs; he pulled her to him as their heavy eyelids fought to stay open. They were both asleep before another word or glance had passed between them. She was nestled entirely into him with her head on his good shoulder. This one more day of existence without death and destruction was all they could wish for, and they were grateful.

Gyttja awoke before Panothos; neither had moved a muscle throughout the still and quiet night.

The moon hovered low in the sky, silently witnessing the calm stillness of the very early morning hour. She carefully untangled herself from Panothos' warm embrace, trying not to disturb his well-deserved rest. The others in the group still slept soundly, nestled in and under the ox carts and inside makeshift tents. She stared down at Panothos as he lay sleeping, wondering how lucky she must be to have her life now intertwined with such a strong and brave man.

Years prior, she had briefly contemplated taking poison and ending her life in captivity, but lacked the courage to go through with it. Life was hard, but she hoped the suffering might recede and give way to moments of some happiness. She couldn't imagine how her feelings could be so different now, unlike that moment so long-ago considering suicide as her only escape. Here with hope in her heart and Panothos by her side, she felt there was finally a reason to wake up every morning.

She felt flushed; maybe the emotional intensity of so many days running had left her ill; possibly, she had slept too long in one position, and the blood had settled unhealthily. She draped one of the pelts around her naked body and quickly ran outside the tent to cool off. Sigrun was outside, stoking the fire and staring up at the star-filled sky.

She looked at Gyttja with a concerned look in her eyes.

"Do you feel ok, Gyttja? You don't look well?"

"I don't know; I awoke feeling dizzy."

Sigrun was several years older than Gyttja; she smirked.

"Why do you smirk at my suffering?"

Sigrun shook her head and smiled. "It is nothing …"

Gyttja quipped, "No, say what you think."

"You have given yourself to Panothos, have you not?"

Gyttja smiled with a shade of embarrassment in her glance. "Yes, he is kind and gentle; I have grown fond of our moments together."

"Silly girl," Sigrun quietly scoffed.

"Why do you call me silly?"

"You really don't know, do you?"

Gyttja looked at Sigrun with a puzzled look. "I don't know what?"

"You have been together more than once now with Panothos?"

"Why is that your business?" Gyttja clapped back.

"You carry his seed, you stupid girl."

Gyttja looked at her, puzzled again. "His seed?"

"Yes, girl, you carry his child; I have seen it in you for many days."

Gyttja gasped. She had never even contemplated such a thought.

"You mean I am ..."

"Yes, you are with child, but you are such a naive thing. You cannot see it, but you have the glow."

Gyttja stood up quickly and ran behind the tent; she squatted and vomited all the contents in her belly into the matted grass. She gained her composure and rose back up; Sigrun smiled at her. "See, I told you, you carry his child, sweet girl; you will be a mother soon if we make it out of this wilderness alive."

Gyttja sat down exasperatedly and joined Sigrun, who continued stoking the campfire. Gyttja stared up into the sky, watching the molten embers decomposing into inert floating ash and wafting away in the breeze, silently contemplating.

Sigrun whispered to Gyttja under her breath, "Such is life."

After a good night of rest, Panothos rose and told everyone to pack up the camp. They would ride hard to seek the place on the trail that led to the village; they would seek the banks the elder mentioned. Once there, they would try to buy peaceful access to the mouth of the mighty river from the leader of the remote village.

This morning, there was no jovial tone in the camp. They knew that the next few days would be a complete backtrack into the probable direction of their enemy. They were losing their strength, and their numbers were diminished. Each time they made contact with the enemy, they lost valuable people. Each time they went to battle, they lost a good friend and a member of their new family.

They had to get far enough fast enough to shake their pursuers, or they would be tormented relentlessly into eventual oblivion. They now moved back in the direction they had just traversed. They were losing ground that had already been gained with every ounce of sweat and blood they could conjure.

They traveled both day and night through fog, mist, and rain. The wagons in the caravan moved through thick grasslands like they were dragging stones and bottomed out in muddy ruts, repeatedly having to be pulled out by men and beasts. They drove the carts forward relentlessly day and night until the fourth morning. They topped a hill and saw the ground rise in the distance as it floated in the air beyond the descending ridge. The illusion finally gave way when they came down into the valley where the village was nestled and could finally see the source of the illusion; the earth was reflecting off the still water.

As before, when they entered this village, there were elders, children, and only a few very young women, not even of an age to breed yet. All the middle-aged people were nowhere to be seen at this remote outpost. Panothos and the group rode to the center of the village and spotted an old one-eyed man walking with a staff; he came out of his hut nervously to greet them. He spoke in broken Persian mixed with some guttural slang that none could understand.

Panothos summoned Ashkan to the front of the procession to translate. The village elder, Araxes, spoke to Ashkan in his broken Persian dialect, instantly realizing by his accent and features that Ashkan was not the same race as the others ... He knew a damn Persian when he saw one and spit at his feet disapprovingly, cursing in his native tongue, judging by the sounds he was making.

Ashkan embarrassedly bowed in submission to the old man, apologizing in Persian for misleading him, then rose back up. He began translating the man's words to Panothos with his head bowed low, not making eye contact with either man. The elder explained, "A very obscenely decorated cruel Persian commander took my wife and daughter into captivity many years ago; I led a revolt against the empire to try and get my wife and daughter back.

"I lost my eye in the battle; they returned with a vengeance and decimated our once thriving village. With so many warriors dying, it shrunk our population by hundreds, and now it is just the weakest of us left. Our once-strong militia was defeated, and the Persian soldiers took our families as human property to sell at bazaars around their foul empire. They force-marched our women and young girls into military camps in the desert and abused them as they saw fit!"

He broke down and cried momentarily, thinking of his wife and daughter's grim fate, before regaining his composure and finishing his story.

"For such devout men who claim to be disciples of the gods, they are still truly barbaric animals! Despicable as any group of lawless soldiers that ever walked this vulgar world! They were unwavering in their cruelty and knew they were cleansing us of any future for our family names!

"We were told that the women were made to languish in the military brothels until they succumbed to the abuse or disease. Some just ran into the desert, never to be seen again. They must have reasoned it was a better fate to die of exposure to the elements rather than live the deplorable future these Persian tyrants offered them!"

Araxes repeatedly spit in the dirt in disgust. At the same time, he furiously spoke of the Persian hordes, scowling with hatred at the mere subject of them, and now, seeing one of their clan members right here standing before him, he was infuriated as if it had all just happened yesterday.

Panothos bowed to the elder and asked him for help. He told the old man he could pay them with Persian spoils. Araxes was skeptical, but when Panothos raised the chain mail bag, he instantly recognized it as a Persian tribute bag.

He said to Panothos, "If you stole that from the Persians, who stole it from the world, I will happily accept this tribute. We will help you as much as possible but with this one precondition! Any Persian soldiers you cross in the future, you must promise me, and I mean you promise me now on your honor, to let no one man in their ranks live! You must leave not a single Persian survivor, none ... period!"

Ashkan looked up and stuttered as the old man spoke; the old man cut his eye, spit at him again, and yelled at him, "Finish saying my words; do not leave any out, and do not stutter!" Ashkan did as he was told ... Araxes then turned and hobbled to the inlet with Panothos in tow to show him what the Persians had left intact after their last incursion. The boy trembled; he felt the old man's one eye murdering him repeatedly throughout the encounter. With each glance, he could feel the hatred and utter contempt tearing away at his soul. Ashkan was sure he would not make it through the night if left alone with these people for even a moment. He imagined that he would be savagely tortured to death or murdered in his sleep. He stuck close to Gyttja and Panothos so he would not be subjected to more of the man's browbeating or fall victim to the village's just cause of vengeance.

The Spartans, who would now forge their way north, knew very little of shipbuilding, only what some of the Greek men had taught them in Persepolis, and they needed to figure out what to do with these half-finished boats. They were warriors capable of making great weapons and training people to use them, but carpentry was not embedded in their knowledge base. The Greek men understood this; they left them to the sacred duty of defense.

Some of the Greek men with Panothos were tradesmen when they weren't fighting invading armies. Panothos instructed a few of these men to accompany them and give counsel. The villagers showed them many unfinished vessels in the inlet that they could use with a little work. A few were already docked in the bay and almost seaworthy; some boats needed their sails pulled and the block and tackle systems threaded.

The men of the group and the old villagers got to work at once, braiding hemp and getting the vessels ready. Araxes began helping the Spartans in the forge, making weapons with Aurias; he pounded shields to aid the Spartan cause. He worked as hard as any of the young men. His ultimate goal? He wanted cruel retribution against the empire that had done nothing but heap injustices on his people for decades; he wanted blood for blood!

The Greeks prepared the new crafts for their mission; they stocked them with weapons and provisions, and the old fishermen created improvised navigational tools and showed them how to read each type. Some of the Greeks knew sailing from growing up in fishing villages themselves. The men who knew carpentry disassembled the carts and packed some of the components in the hulls; they would need the wheels and axles again once upriver.

Strategically, enough wood on the boats could be repurposed into carts once they reached their desired portage. One of the boats was large enough to bring a few horses and two teams of oxen on board; it had a substantial hold in the hull's center. The wooden cages were initially intended for prisoners of war or hauling slaves but were large enough for beasts of burden.

The new crafts the villagers gave them were fairly agile, steady in the deep or shallow draft, crested with intimidating carvings of serpents high on their bows, perfect for battle, fishing, or just speed. They maneuvered by sail on open waters or could be propelled by oars on the rivers; whatever was needed, they were very versatile vessels.

After days of hard work, the group pushed the new boats off their moorings and into the deep-water inlet. They waved to Araxes and the others as they watched them cast off. Araxes stared, full of hope that these travelers would inflict significant and permanent damage on their soulless shared enemy. He walked down the pier, waving until he saw Ashkan sitting on the stern of the first vessel; he spat one more time in his direction, then stopped abruptly to take in the view.

Araxes prayed they would have great success; he, too, would make offerings to the gods that night for complete domination over this malignant and vicious enemy.

Gyttja enjoyed the beauty and bounty of this inland waterway. She spent her time netting fish and collecting and storing fresh water from the sails in earthen pottery donated by the villagers. Through squalls of stinging rain or the occasional windless, hot day, they passed undetected through the vast waterway until they reached the inlet of the Volga River, where the waters went from clear and saline to muddy and fresh. Rather than get out and find their bearings at the mouth of the great river, the boats turned down their sails. They went straight to oar, meandering up the mouth of the river due northeasterly into its vast twisting waterway; like a marauding horde, they dug in and pushed on with all the strength they could muster.

Gyttja looked at Panothos with great big eyes and a warm smile. She did not say it aloud, but she could vividly remember passing by this place as a child on her journey east to the palace of her enslavement. The two colors of water uniquely formed a distinct line; it was unmistakable. She remembered wondering about this as she passed here as a child. What force could cause water to form such a sharp line of separation? One thing was for sure; they were moving in the direction of her childhood, closer to the vast lands of her family. She rejoiced inside because she felt she might have a chance to see the shores of her homeland again.

Tyranos, in the back of the second boat, spent the whole time in the inland sea vomiting violently over the stern rail. Before the head injury, he had never felt this sickness in the open water, but now, hereafter the injury, he could not find his balance and just held on to the side of the boat, retching and laying his head on the trim. The open water had not agreed with him, but now they would put oars in the water and push themselves upstream against the current. He hoped the arduous physical task would strengthen his resolve and restore his sea legs. That the physical movement would cement his gut and give him the needed focus.

Sigrun brought him fresh water and dry bread to restore his composure. They all knew he could do the work of two men without complaint, and when put to a task, he would not be undone! The beast in the cells in the ship's hull made this one slower in the water than the other two vessels. Tyranos put his head down and selflessly concentrated on doing what needed to get done; he took an oar by himself in the front of the boat and pulled his way upstream for all his worth, inspiring the other pairs of rowers to push hard upstream. With hands blistered and bleeding, they pulled at the oars for three days, and the vessels cut like blades through the water. They made astonishingly good distance for a flotilla of wounded and battered warriors. Finally, after much effort, they landed the boats on the bank and made camp at the narrows Araxes had spoken of.

Panothos gathered his men and asked them to share their thoughts and concerns about his plan. They were all free again, and choices were guaranteed to free men who were active in their pursuit of liberty, and now, they intended to stay this way at all costs. The same rights would be assured to the women who accompanied them on the journey; they fought bravely alongside the men, shields in tow. There would be no such thing as ownership of a human with this group, not after the captivity they had collectively endured ... except Ashkan; he was indentured until they knew for sure that they were far enough away and would be free of the Persian menace. Once his bill was paid to Panothos and the Greeks, he too would be freed.

It was a way of honor to adhere to these principles; once your word is pledged, you must follow its mandate through to the end. This was a stalwart of the concept of freedom: that reasonable choices were always available to individuals at any moment; if your choices were not good, there was no one to blame but yourself. Panothos was a man of his word, so he earnestly spoke to them all by the fire that night.

"My friends, my brothers and sisters, my new family ... We are all bonded in sacrifice as one entity by these many trials we have endured.

"I asked you to guard my back and pledged to you that I would guard yours.

"I asked you to trust me in military matters, and you have agreed with my strategies, and due to your strength and bravery, we have repeatedly persevered and gone so much farther than I honestly ever imagined we would.

"Throughout this ordeal, we are proving ourselves worthy ... every ... single ... day! Giving every ounce of energy and having unwavering trust in one another, ensuring that we will forge a future free from servitude and cowardly disgraces ...

"I asked of you to sacrifice your very lives to serve our freedom, and all of you obliged freely and did so with great honor.

"Some of our brothers and sisters have fallen in battle and become martyrs to our cause; they gave their lives without complaint or question. We will humbly feast by their side in the Pantheon one day and celebrate their endeavors, proving to them that their blood was not spilled in vain. For their sacrifice, we are forever indebted.

"But now, I will ask all of you who are still here with us for one more sacrifice, for I have one more very important request ...

"I ask you to attempt to vanish with me into a new life that holds none of the mementos of the days behind us ...

"From this day forth, I ask you to erase your former life and begin anew ... in a land where none of you men have ever stepped foot, and some of you girls can barely remember.

"We shall convert to a simple lifestyle, the lifestyle of fishermen, farmers, and artist ... a far stretch from the battlefields and bosom of our beloved Mother Greece. Though we will keep our defenses strong, we will not exist solely by the sword. We will be nothing more than a caravan of ghosts moving silently up a river. We will move like fog and make our home where the winter nights are long."

He paused and looked at them all with a solemn stare …

"Because this is our fate … and the alignment of the stars has birthed us into this struggle, not of our choice, but it makes us bound by the necessity to carry one another through these exacting trials."

Panothos believed that the idea of the gods was just an instrument of control humans had recklessly created to their detriment. An omnipotent, untouchable being placed on the surface of the psyche so the rich and powerful could keep the superstitious masses in line to keep them from wanting to grab too much power from those currently wielding it.

The gods, Panothos deliberated, were entirely irrelevant to any outcome. He had witnessed their impotence firsthand. Since the will of the gods dictated every fragment of life, Panothos repeatedly tried to hear their voices in his mind, but they were consistently and ominously silent. He tried to comprehend their wisdom but saw no wisdom therein. He tried to honor their nature, but their nature was always perverse, twisted, and utterly absent of humanity … Maybe Gyttja's gods had more to say than the silent ancient gods of Sparta; this, he hoped.

They said only the priests could communicate with the gods directly, and priests were just power-hungry, incestuous slobs who ruled with much the same power as kings. They were known to covet earthly pleasures and steal treasure just as the rest of the people; they were just more shamelessly underhanded than the average man and would dogmatically prey on the average man's fears and weakness … But as many around him believed fervently in the gods, he invoked them to help make his point clearly and inspire hope.

"What I propose is a very bold step indeed. We have pushed hard for so many days moving up this river, and I assume we are still many days from our intended destination? I believe in my bones that the way to our new home is not on this river but instead where the sun recedes behind the sky every night, across these vast unknown lands of thatched roof villages and peasant fields. Across the unknown hills and valleys that will take us to the cold lands to our north. We will convert our boats into carts, and the remaining horses will pull our carts like we're farmers, and we will not overtly show our true strength; we will try to avoid being seen as a fighting force. We will shed our old gods and adopt their new ones, the same as ours in everything but name.

"From this day forth, we are only humble souls searching for safe passage.

"How say you all?"

The group looked around at each other to seek reassurance that they were all thinking the same thing. Then Tyranos stood and proclaimed, "I am your blade, sir; I am your weapon!"

Aurias raised his fist into the air and also proclaimed, "I am your shield, sir; I am the eyes in your back!"

The rest of the group mumbled to themselves. The idea of never returning to Greece was alarming, but alone in this foreign wilderness, they were nothing better than a simple meal for a bear or wolf pack. Gyttja stood up before Aristos or any of the Greeks had a chance to speak.

She exclaimed loudly, "I am your flame, sir; I illuminate your path, am your light, and I would freely give my life in service to thee!"

All the others, feeling some trepidation for their delayed response, followed suit in a unified oath. "We are your phalanx and will pierce the hearts of our enemies!" And so, they stayed the course of Panothos' choosing. They would follow him to the grave if that were the way it was to be! He was now officially their leader and commander. They were without a country, but they were unified in their objectives. They were a force to be reckoned with, even with such small numbers, and at this point, they had nothing to lose in embracing this resistance.

As the Greeks disassembled the boats, Panothos sent Aurias and Tyranos in two directions, scouting and hunting along the north and northwest frontier's forest. As they converted the boats into carts, they built hidden compartments underneath the carriages to house the many weapons they had constructed back in the village. This way, they could travel stealthily along as migrating travelers or traders and avoid being left in a position of weakness if provoked.

They would trim down the sails and drape them over frames again to offer shelter for a portion of the group as they rested; they would start traveling in rolling shifts again to make up for the time spent rebuilding. *This schedule should also compensate for the days lost backtracking*, thought Panothos. But he knew that Governor Hamedani's group was possibly not the only outfit sent to capture them; his senses tingled as he stayed on high alert to look for signs of trackers or more assassins.

The Greeks toiled and built more robust carts, able to navigate over rocks and through dirt and mud. They melted the anchors and forged the iron into sheets to reinforce the wheels so they might hold together through the rough terrain without breaking apart. When the work was complete, one could not tell that these carts were once sailing vessels or armored, except for the depth of the tracks left imprinted in the loose dirt. Only such a heavy wagon would displace so much dirt as it passed; this could not be avoided, and only a very experienced tracker would know this as a sign of an armored wagon.

A few days passed, and Aurias and Tyranos returned with reconnaissance information on the best possible path to advance. They smoked fish and meat and dried the pelts to sustain them on the next leg of their escape. They were warned that the places they were going were as cold as the mountains they crossed weeks before. They would need these many pelts and good fortune to keep from freezing to death under the bitter clear northern nights. Tyranos slayed a bear during his excursion; he wore the claws and teeth around his neck as a trophy and would use its thick fur to stay warm. His hair was becoming long again, and his beard was thick, with gray hairs beginning to show. He was reasonably young, but his years on this planet were full of hard-fought battles that earned him these discolorations ... It was said that a man who endures such hardship in battle could have his hair turn gray overnight.

As Panothos looked around the encampment, he noticed they had all come to resemble mountain men and vagabonds, like homeless, bedraggled travelers. They only saw their reflections in pools of water from time to time when they bathed; this was not a bad thing, he surmised; after all, the Persians were looking for soldiers, but now they had come to resemble a group of beleaguered pilgrims.

Aurias found a cart path that led to the Northwest. He only saw peasant shacks and farmlands surrounded by lush forests on this route. Tyranos had only encountered thick wilderness due North, no people or trails. With the new heavy carts, Panothos decided it best to follow the cart path and try to move quickly; all agreed that this would make the most sense. They set out as the sun rose in the eastern sky at their backs. The morning was rich with dew, cicadas, and calling birds forming a cacophony of summer sounds. The scent of the forest changed from dry cedar to arboreal; the shrill rattle of cicadas ramped up at times into a deafening crescendo and then subsided into random chattering. Water dripped from the leaves of the trees as the sun began to warm the woods around them. The air was thick with humidity and smelled of leaves composting on the forest floor. The carts rattled as they rolled down the pathway.

The horses were not packhorses and had to be constantly made to work together and find a cadence. The women gnawed on leather while the soldiers in the wagons slept in shifts. Panothos and Aurias scouted ahead as Gyttja watched the rear of the pack and lingered behind at times to listen for

the movement of enemy scouts. So far, they had
been lucky and met no resistance on this trail. No
warlords, militias, or robbers had made their
presence known to the group, and none of the very
few traders they passed had mentioned anything of
a significant movement of soldiers.

The battle chest was now the only coin that
Panothos used at trading posts along the trail to
buy mead and wine. They knew better than to trust
the drinking water in these lands that could make a
man so sick he would beg for death to take him in
the night to alleviate the suffering in his bowels.
They slogged night and day for weeks with very few
stops along the way to rest the animals. Dialects
changed, and the land flattened into vast prairies
dotted with small beaver ponds.

The mosquitos and deerflies became an
unrelenting nuisance; Gyttja would ask Panothos to
stop occasionally, making salves with ash, tallow,
cow urine, and mint leaves to keep the tiny
persistent monsters at bay. Night and day swarms
began to form around the horses and men, making
everyone crazy with their incessant buzzing and
biting itch. They burned dry dung at the
procession's lead to keep the insects outside their
perimeter. Many of the Arcadians thought they had
made the wrong choice coming here to this
unrelenting and hostile land. They remembered the
food from Xerxes palace and wondered if Spartan

pride was just too much and that these men did not realize a good thing when they had it. But they had chosen to follow Panothos, and they would find a way to make the best of it.

Days turned to weeks as the daylight hours got shorter. It was sometime near the end of summer, and they had seen no evidence that the Persians were in active pursuit. The trail they were following was a desolate one. This path only appeared to be well traveled in the earlier sections. Now, it was a deserted wilderness path, with its direction becoming, at times, unapparent and unforgivingly damaging to the carts. Occasionally, they had to go long distances around swamps and small lakes, only to scout for days to find another leg of the long unused northward trail again. The game had become small and lean; only rabbits, rodents, and an occasional freshwater fish from a beaver pond were harvested.

The countryside stretched for days unchanging. The horses, not accustomed to this mundane type of repetitive labor, were restless and fought, wounding each other with large bites. These were no pack horses but war horses being stifled into manual labor, much like the Spartan men now becoming porters rather than soldiers; this made for awkward moments of silence when Aurias and Tyranos would stare into the abyss of the campfire and wonder how they would train themselves and their minds for docile, domesticated life. They had known only one purpose, war ... and for so long now, the day-to-day rituals of mundane existence began to dull their senses and sully their brave hearts. Panothos had the companionship of Gyttja, but Aurias and Tyranos only busied themselves with the maintenance and logistics of traveling and how to best defend the group against ambush.

They had been moving steadily for over a month, but this morning, an unexpected heavy fog rapidly set in; it made the air like liquid. They could see the air swirl as they disturbed it in passing. For hours, Aurias inched his scouts forward silently. In the dense fog, they were trying to stay on the trail. Sounds stirred the imagination, playing tricks on the men's minds. They could hear the echo of men speaking and laughter, but nothing was visible. They stopped to listen, not moving, breathing lightly to hear these apparitions. Everyone in the wagons woke up and waited for directions. The scouts crept forward with their swords drawn, then knelt and observed. The sound changed from muted to vast ... But they could only see the cloud they were in. But then, like the breath of a ghost, a calm wind began to offer itself, and the sky brightened; the dense gray fog began dissipating right in front of them just as abruptly as it had shrouded them, retreating into the forest they had emerged, like the faint deception of a witch nearby.

As the foreground showed itself, Aurias and his scouts found themselves on a high ridgeline looking down on the outskirts of a massive outpost. There were no fortress walls but a sprawling city of tents, tiny shacks, and what looked like a traveling bazaar. Inside and around it, they could see indications of a significant population of nomads. Whoever they were, they did not live in fear and left a mark on the land with their mere presence.

The scouts immediately circled back and warned Panothos, who had stopped the procession earlier in the morning as the fog descended on them.

He gathered a small portion of the group and went to investigate. They approached cautiously, still resembling beggars, walking in directly through a gap in the tents that seemed like a gateway or a proper entrance. The Greeks could understand portions of an ancient unwritten Thracian dialect that these rough-looking people were speaking.

They believed these must be Cimmerians or at least a scattered ancient tribe of them. They thought they existed only in myth, boisterous herdsmen who drank heavily and had no allegiance to any exulted flag or king. They were rumored to travel in caravans and lived in harmony with nature. They relocated their camps around the territory with the changing seasons and followed the herd migrations.

Panothos and the men entered a small makeshift Tavern and were able to order wine. The Great Teacher Lycurgus taught Thracian and the roots of the Cimmerians language, which was the crude guttural dialect he heard them speaking. Many of their phrases were used by Greek writers of old. Panothos had been a student at some of the cults of Lycurgus symposiums as he trained as a young man to become a warrior. When they met, they recited the timeline of battles and the philosophies and bloodline of the Thracians.

The tavern owner brought out pork from the spit, which was never served while they had been interred in Persia. They ate and sipped the harsh wines while the tribesmen spoke and whispered and gossiped about the stranger's presence in the camp. There was an electrical charge in the air; Panothos could hear a group in the corner speaking of a large fortification of men less than an hour's journey from where they now drank. They said a large foreign army was dug in, a thousand strong. Panothos walked up to the table and introduced himself to the men. The men were apprehensive and cut eyes at Panothos and the other Spartans. He pulled aside his robe's sleeve and showed the men the shoulder and upper torso wounds. He exclaimed, "The men who did this to me were Persians. I believe the men in the camp you speak of are the same! What say you?"

The men were astonished at the brazen way Panothos had introduced himself and his unusual accent; he spoke to them even though he got no reply.

"And?"

One of the men who seemed to be a leader, a large man with a mane of matted hair, finally spoke up and asked, "Who do you think you are to come into our tavern house asking questions and blaming those you did not know the whereabouts of prior?"

"Why do you camp on the opposing side of us and this large army? Are you all just scouts or spies for this large army?"

Suddenly, most of the men in the tavern drew their blades and became very interested in the men's conversation. Panothos and the two Spartans raised their arms and showed they were unarmed. The room relaxed for a moment, and Panothos began to speak.

"Those soldiers in the camp are our sworn enemies. They come to your homeland like locusts and take what they please. Only old men and young children were in the last two villages we traveled through. The middle-aged have been sold into slavery or worse! We stand against this army of opportunistic thieves."

The large man laughed out loud as the rest of the room snickered ... "You and your few travelers

194

plan to take on this vast army to your east ... really?"
"What large balls you must have." Laughter erupted
all around again.

"What makes you think you can beat these
soldiers? You soldier, traveler, spy, or whatever you
truly are?"

Panothos pulled from under his garments the
war purse he had taken from Governor Hamedani.
He threw it onto the table, and the room instantly
went silent. These men knew well of these bags.
They were sent the bags on occasion to pay tribute.
The elders always warned of the great Persian
army of the south, that it was better to pay tribute to
their emissaries than to cross swords with their
cavalry. They had paid tribute to the Governor of
Sardis, so why was this large group of invaders now
encamped in their lands?

"How did you get that bag?" The large man
shouted at Panothos. Since their cover was blown
and they needed help, Panothos told them of the
battle so fresh behind them and the victory that
gave them these spoils of war. He opened the bag
and spilled the remaining coins on the table. The
large man grasped one of the rolled coins before
him and sneered as he inspected it.

"This is one of our coins! Where did you get
this from? Please tell me again!" Standing now in a
confrontational stance.

Panothos exclaimed, "We took it from Governor Hamedani, one of the retreating commanders of the Persian force we decimated many weeks ago!"

The large man clenched the coin in his hand and frowned. He paced and turned his head and shook it in disapproval. This was going to be trouble; he muttered under his breath to the others in a slang that Panothos did not recognize.

The soldiers camped on the outskirts of their land had accepted tribute just after the last migration; it seemed they must now be back in these great numbers to ask for even more tribute! This was absolutely unacceptable.

He asked Panothos, "What do you intend to do about this situation that 'you' have created here?"

Panothos said in a low growl, "I intend to cut the hearts out of every last one of these men so I can move peacefully through to the lands of the north." The large man smirked, then smiled and asked, "Do you have weapons?" Panothos nodded.

The large man told Panothos he might bring his small band of travelers to the gathering, and they would join them in a feast the following night. Panothos asked inquisitively, "A feast?" The man replied ... "Yes, our night before a battle feast. On the morrow of the feast, we will crush these foreign invaders for so blatantly disrespecting the terms of our agreed-upon tribute."

Panothos reached out to shake the large man's arm and spoke up. "All the spoils of this battle are yours. We want to fight alongside you and kill these invaders who seek to take our heads."

The large chieftain laughed and raised his goblet in the air, smiling and proclaiming, "As if you ever really had any choice in these matters!"

The following night, the tents were full of herdsmen and Greeks. Boar roasted on spits over open fires as men tended and basted the meat with herbs, wine, and lemon. They smoked pipes of hemp and tobacco, telling stories of their great exploits in far-off lands. This feast was the best food the Greeks had eaten in so very long; it resembled the grand festivals at home. Wine and mead spilled into the glasses as men raised toasts to one another's bravery in the looming battle. Whole tables in the grand tent in the center would erupt into song, roaming rowdily in and out of key. Men wrestled for sport in the room's dark corners as rough women chose certain warriors to take back to their tents and molest. The nomadic herdsman knew how to throw a party; it was almost like home but still a world away from anyone they knew. The food and drink flowed freely until the moon hung like a jeweled ornament in the bosom of the star-filled sky. Men made their way to the outskirts of the camp and fell asleep in a drunken stupor. Knowing the animosity of the enemy lurking in the periphery, the Greeks drank only the watered-down children's wine. They feasted on the fatty dripping meats and flatbreads to fill their bellies with a decent meal that was not rabbit or venison. Tomorrow, the energy would be needed to finish this once and forever. To stop running and start living again, to move past this moment of desperation and forge ahead with a new life in a new land. But first, they must tempt the creator by attacking a division of abused Persian soldiers who feared for their lives from their upper ranks and the enemy. Only after the wager is sealed with the Pride and the bloody stain of victory would Panothos and his men ever know the gentler side of a peaceful life, and its delicate reprieve, or they would honorably accept the last breaths of a warrior's proud demise. One thing for certain: they would not allow themselves to be taken captive by Xerxes again.

Chapter 8

Dead Reckoning

It was a gray and humid morning. It felt as if a storm was about to roll in; the wind was beginning to pick up, vividly changing from the stagnant night's moist blanketing of fog. The Greeks roused early to get the upper hand on the day, but when they arose, one hundred or so of the herdsmen encircled their tents facing with their spear tips pointing inward at them. Panothos slowly rose to his feet and approached the guards before him. "Why do you surround us like this?"

A guard pointed to a shadowy figure approaching from out of the darkness. A very old woman in wolf furs, adorned in ornamental carved human bones, slowly came forward. She had tattoos of ancient symbols on the wrinkled skin around her eyes. She resembled a witch, and of this, there was no doubt ...

She exclaimed, "Silence!"

Panothos looked at the woman inquisitively, staring straight into her beady, aged eyes.

"Do ye think a people so vast as we are run only by oafs and brutes? We are the proud people of the Steppes. We have endured for thousands of years and will remain for thousands more. We will watch your empires be born, grow tall, and then bend and crumble ... just as we have for all the ages."

"Don't ye feel prideful as I send my sons to die for their people. I am the mother of this tribe, and you will seek only to live or die by my words."

"These Persian barbarians have come to our lands without tribute or my permission; they have come to us here seeking vengeance, it seems!" "And why, may I ask, should I view your people as any different?"

"We have aligned our visions with a pact against a common enemy, but what more do you have to offer in order for me to know your 'real' intention honestly, Oh ye' Spartans and Greeks?"

Panothos felt a rush of adrenaline shoot through every cell of his body, so much so that he could taste the essence of metal in his saliva.

He glanced at Tyranos and Aurias; they had the same stoic expression on their faces as he, but they, too, were in a state of utter and complete shock.

"Don't ye' think ye' can fool me now, boy. Soldiers, you are! Not humble travelers, but killers who creep in the night!"

"We will fight with the likes of you, but we will do so only on our terms; we will not negotiate our offers with deceptive rogues like yourselves; you will get what you get as we allow!"

The large chieftain from the Tavern the night before approached, kneeled, and bowed before the old witch. She touched his head, patted him on the cheek, and then walked slowly forward to her white horse; he helped her up into her saddle. She then slowly rode with her guards to the exit of the encampment.

The large man threw shackles on the dirt before the Spartan's feet and belched orders to them.

"Put these on ... do it now so you may fight this battle with us today!"

Panothos asked, "What is the meaning of this ... you said we would fight this battle together."

The large warrior replied, "We will let you fight, but it will be on our terms ... do as we say, and you will have your battle!"

The three men reluctantly picked up the chains and put their wrists in the clasped irons; herdsmen pinned them closed around their wrists. Panothos and the others were apprehensive about putting themselves in bondage yet again; they wondered if these people could be trusted. They followed the direction of the chieftain, and all submitted to the instructions he had given. They marched forward until they caught up to the old witch's guard. The large man hurried the three

Spartans still further away from the others and marched them directly behind the witch's horse; she turned and looked down at Panothos.

"You will go with us now chained as captives, but you will finish the day as the warriors you are rumored to be."

They marched behind the witch's horse for some time, etching a trail in the heavy morning dew. The wind wildly moved the billowing grasses on the prairie back and forth, like gentle waves rolling across a vast grain ocean. The prairie seemed to go on forever until it met the sky on the endless horizon.

After some travel, they stopped briefly on the outskirts of what looked to be the vast Persian encampment they were planning to attack. Panothos and Aurias traded glances, wondering how this would play out.

The remaining Greeks and Gyttja approached behind them, wearing the same attire as the Cimmerians. Behind the Spartans, Cimmerian Guards slowly moved them forward at the tip of small curved swords. Suddenly, all sheathing them in unison once they approached the witch and her entourage and halted in step.

Gyttja yelled to Panothos in Greek, "I have your weapons!"

Panothos nodded to her, and the procession started making its way down the worn path in the direction of the entrance to the Persian camp. Panothos wondered if the herdsman would double-cross them or if this was all just a ploy to catch the camp off guard with such brilliant pageantry.

The witch and the large man broke away from the formation with the three Spartans in tow on foot behind their mounts. The central column of Cimmerian guards stopped and maintained their ranks with the girls and the Greek men two rows back, buried deep inside their formation. They approached two large fires on either side of the entrance to the Persian camp. A few words were spoken between the chieftain and one of the guards, who immediately ran inside the camp to fetch someone of higher rank. A figure stomped up the pathway through the tents and up to the front of the procession, where the Spartans stood in bondage. Samid Al Sahan suddenly appeared, smirking as he approached the witch's entourage.

The witch spoke to Samid in Persian, saying, "Oh, great commander, we have found these slaves for your purchase!"

"Men of real stature to strengthen your army … warriors disguised in pilgrim cloths. We found these retches hiding in our lands. What bounty do you offer? What will you pay for these slaves we wish to trade?

What have you for us?"

Samid approached the three Spartans and spoke to them in Greek, "You miserable cowards! You took the great care and generosity of King Xerxes for granted and spit on his boots with your little misguided adventure. You spilled the blood of many Persian soldiers on our lands, yet here you stand before me now, beaten and in bondage again. Greatness ... I see no greatness; all I see are miserable failures before me, shackled in irons ..."

"You are not even soldiers anymore! You are only gamblers with enormously good luck. You deserve to be executed in the day's light, right here before me, but Xerxes is a fool and wants to know what creates your hubris. He wishes you returned to him with your hearts still beating."

Panothos gritted his teeth and nodded. He wanted to feel his blade slice through this man's heart and watch his liquid spill onto the muddy ground.

The witch exclaimed, "Until you grant tribute to our people, these men are not yours. You will come to our camp to take them tonight when you bring us our tribute!"

Samid replied with a forceful tone, "Who are you to dictate the terms of this exchange? I want them all, and I will have them now! I represent the hand of the omnipotent master Xerxes, ruler of all kingdoms!"

"You will take my terms as I see fit to give them!"

Samid told his personal guard to fetch Governor Hamedani, "Tell him to bring my war chest; bring it here immediately!" He told another soldier to fetch him a runner. He wanted to get a message back to Xerxes to tell him that the escaped prisoners were now captured and in his possession. The runner approached and confirmed his verbal orders. He mounted a stallion, whipping it as it bolted south in a full gallop back towards Persepolis, sprinting in the distance with his dispatch faithfully memorized.

The old witch smiled and replied, "As you wish to believe, you may."

The morning sunbeams peaked out cautiously just behind the tops of the far-rolling hills, revealing the coming day in small cloud-shrouded glimpses. However, the heavy gray overcast sky had set in, overshadowed the peaceful morning, and would not let its light ultimately shine through; it was just a diffused glow with a dull gray ambiance. Occasionally, you could hear thunder rumbling in the western sky, echoing in the surrounding hills with an almost rolling resonance. Hamedani approached the informal meeting with Raza Douul and his personal guard with a war chest in tow. Samid motioned to Hamedani to stop short as he questioned the witch.

"Where are the rest of the men and slaves I seek?"

"The others who undoubtedly trespass uninvited on your lands?"

The old woman retorted, "You mean the same as your men who have trespassed here so unwelcome?"

"I have them many in my camp. What could you want with them? They are misfits, vagabonds, and whores ... I plan to sell the whores to the brothels of the clans in the east for large pieces of gold, and I will sell the men to go and work in the mines in the North ... what is it to you?"

"You have in front of you what we negotiated!"

Samid shook his head in disbelief. He gestured to Hamedani, told him to take out a small portion of the gold within, and showed it to the witch's guard.

"And how much for the rest of your captives? What sort of bounty will you ask me to give back the rest of '*my*' prisoners?"

The witch replied, "We want All of it!"

Samid laughed and again shook his head.

"All of it?"

Again, closer and even more frequently, the thunder rumbled and rolled ferociously behind the dark clouds in the western sky.

"All of it!" she replied willfully.

"All of it?"

Samid shook his head in disbelief. Who does she think she is? He thought to himself. What could pervert a herdsman's thoughts into such a false sense of empowerment? How dare she try to assert demands on a Persian commander. What foul delusion must be in her mind to try and wield so much power?

"One hundred pieces of gold should cover it, I would say …" Samid laughingly said to the old witch.

Hamedani laughed at the absurdity of the witch's prideful statements, shaking his head in shocked amazement at her impudence.

A cold, hateful look descended from her glaring eyes. She did not find Samid or Hamedani's Pride at all amusing. She wondered what spirit possessed men so small as this to walk the world with such selfish ambitions, lacking any small portion of humility and underestimating power on such a scale. She wondered what coerces men's souls to try and wield this power so lazily and clumsily with only a nominal understanding of the pillars of honor. Those who think that stone and wood are a match for the water's current falling from the mountain melts or from the sky in small drops of rain … Water moves large stones and earth and is much more formidable than these pathetic actors dressed in fancy garb.

"I said all of it!" she yelled again without flinching.

Repeatedly, the thunder rumbled to the east, shaking the very earth on which they stood. Now, a constant low drone that surged and swayed reverberated around their conversation.

"You stupid cow! You will not extort a Persian Emissary; you will bow to the will of our god-king and beg for his mercy!" he screamed back, now quite agitatedly ...

Closer and closer, the thunder crept until it changed its timbre, almost climaxing into the sound of beating drums, like waves collapsing onto cliffs, colliding violently on the stones of its jagged shore. From every direction, the noise oscillated, surged, and then receded. Then morphed again and again, now beginning to sound ever so familiar ... but still not quite apparent ... the sound of thousands of footsteps like war drums undulating in an ominous cadence devoid of any rhythm.

Samid looked back at the old witch as if questioning, "What have you done to me?"

The witch smiled, again exclaiming, "Maybe you should take back your foolish pride and learn to fear us so-called 'stupid cows,' commander!"

An arrow arched in the sky from behind the witch's procession, piercing Raza Douul through his throat. He fell instantaneously, dropping the war chest and grabbing his neck, immediately going into convulsions and flopping around on the ground like a fish suffocating out of water.

A tent in the back of the Persian camp suddenly exploded high into the air like it was lifted by the winds of a storm. Persian soldiers began scattering in every direction, screaming out in absolute terror. Cimmerian horsemen guided massive stampeding cattle herds directly into the Persian camp. Like an ominous wave of nature's simple fury, they collided headlong with the unprepared Persian soldiers. The bulls in the front of the stampede began wildly trampling everything that stood in their path; the thunder truly had arrived on the plain, exposing the large army's weakness ... pride.

They barreled violently through the center of the encampment, followed by hundreds more, which caved in through the canvass walls of the barrack tents on every side. In a full galloping stampede, tens of thousands of cattle rolling over the ground's contours resembled a flash flood, decimating everything in its path.

Pushing the herd into this frenzy, Cimmerian soldiers on horseback routed the Stampede strategically through the camp's center, where the officer's quarters were located. They fired flaming arrows into the camp's tents, setting off more fires and creating instantaneous chaos on a massive scale. The cool morning air became diffused with a dust cloud that stretched the whole length of the camp and then far beyond.

Gyttja, the remaining Greek warriors, and the large Cimmerian chieftain with his guards in tow ran up and surrounded the three bound Spartans, shielding them from Samid's guards. They planted massive, dripping flaming torches in a crescent around the front of their position to divert the charging beasts narrowly around. Samid and Governor Hamedani turned and looked at one another with an absurd look of bewilderment, frozen in an unsophisticated shock. Stuck between a stampede and a hostile force, they instantly realized their failures and retreated into the chaos of the oncoming stampede.

Gyttja ran up to Panothos; she released the pins that bound the clasps on his wrists. He and the others were now free from bondage, wringing their hands and reaching for their weapons. She handed the Spartans their shields and swords, and then they braced for impact! The witch nodded to Panothos as she exfiltrated behind her guards and departed the area, virtually disappearing before their eyes. She pulled her entourage back to a small knoll outside the camp to orchestrate the carnage firsthand.

Many of the Persian soldiers who were not instantly trampled by the herd had no real chance of survival against the Greeks and herdsmen. Some

Persians ran blindly past the approaching Cimmerian cavalry without engaging in combat with them in their fearful drive to escape from the wild stampeding beasts. They put aside all their military training and were fleeing for their life. The Cimmerian rider's arrows rained down on them, but amid the confusion, the soldiers had not grabbed their shields to defend themselves from this kind of assault. Only some had the clarity of thought to grab a weapon to even start fighting back. As soldiers, they were now useless, becoming cheap fodder for the Greek and Cimmerian assaults. Even the Immortal troops had given in to the fear of the wild beasts; they were not trained to deal with a force of nature like this; no conventional force could imagine this bovine front. The Greek Hoplites advanced through the melee, running up to the Three Spartan's position. They pushed forward in front, guarding them with their shields and torches.

"What is your order, sir?" Arestus belted out.

Panothos pointed his spear to the center of the camp, directly to the place where Samid had chosen to retreat, and he yelled out, "Take back your freedoms; finish them!"

The men, in unison, trudged forward in a tight, crouching formation as crisp as any Spartan force Panothos had commanded. They moved forward in a steady syncopated march, hacking down Samid's personal guard one by one as they rose to make contact and defend their commander. Panothos men finished each kill with an extra twist of the blade or extra death blow for good measure, an unspoken nod to the wishes of the elder Araxes, whose hospitality and generosity had led them to this pivotal moment. Aurias pushed through the Persians like a sharp scythe through young green grass; the small group advanced past rumbling beasts and small patches of resistance. They were setting ablaze anything that would burn. Groups of Persian soldiers retreated in complete disarray to the east through gaps in the stampede, only to be chased down and killed by Cimmerian horsemen who had been waiting in the camp's outer perimeter. The Persian force was being shown the power of the people of the steppes. A herdsman on horseback was as good as any battlefield-tested archer, and to their advantage, they could release their arrows and hit targets even while hanging from the side of a horse, riding bareback. No armored cavalry, such as these riders, could achieve this tactic with graceful agility. The Persians couldn't even see who was firing at them; they only saw the horses approaching and fell with a kill shot through the neck or chest.

Auria's large torso heaved and swayed in the dusty haze of the morning as he swung a battle-axe, circling it in the air and bludgeoning his terrified victims with its pitted but sharp blade and spiked rear hammer wedge. Witnessing such a violent interaction between two humans was an incredible sight. Tyranos hacked his way through to the rear of the Persian fighters and then turned to attack their ranks, consuming them from the inside out. With Greeks on each side of his advance, he cleansed the battlefield of any who may have the will to form a solid resistance.

The Cimmerian herd at this time of the season was massive; wherever the Cimmerians moved, so did their herds. Six clans of them stayed on the plains near the eastern steppes. It just so happened that this was the season that they would all meet to trade animals, negotiate grazing rights, promote their kinsman within the ranks, marry off their daughters, and settle debts and differences in an orderly manner. To attack one clan would be a challenge to any well-trained army. To attack all the clans at once would be a suicidal mistake by even the most sharpened legion. But now, a force of nature that few on this planet would even imagine magnified Samid's error through a prism of failure and into a rapidly evolving, slow-motion catastrophe. Slow, stupid herd animals had scattered and decimated his troops; the Greeks were now approaching on his flank. The usually bold commander was now rendered speechless. He never imagined a docile plant eater would be the catalyst for his ruin. A fucking bull ... it was too simple even to contemplate. As Samid stared into the sky, pondering, Hamedani repeatedly yelled at him! "What now? What now?"

Samid Al Sahan just gazed over the ruins of his army, completely and totally in a state of paralyzed dismay. He resigned himself to the fact that he had been vastly outmaneuvered by Plain's dwellers by this simple force of nature. Governor Hamedani looked on in dismay as this once-great commander dropped to his knees and began resigning his dwindling fate to the gods ... It must be the gods' will, and who was he to try and force the water's current away from where it chose to drop freely? He was now just a grain of sand traveling in the flow, triggered by the motion of the spinning earth, a traveler in the currents of unbiased fate. He thought how queer it was to bow to Xerxes, who was only a man, not at all a God, not even as powerful as the simple Bovine creature that just trampled his ambitions and future firmly into the ground without a shred of malice.

As the moments ground on, the extermination of the Persians continued just as Panothos had promised Araxis. The plan had succeeded; their new ally had pulled them through from what most likely would have been a crushing and vapid defeat to a victory clenched in no uncertain terms. Panothos was well impressed with the old witch's strategy. It was all-encompassing and left nothing to chance. Nature was a variable that no commander could truly master or defend against entirely. At the end of the battle, the Persian camp lay in smoldering ruin; they suffered the same fate as Panothos and the men did at Thermopylae. This time, Panothos showed a complete lack of empathy towards the enemy. He ordered the execution of every wounded Persian soldier where they lay, with no exceptions.

As the day became evening, the totality of the battle showed itself clearly. A makeshift court of tribal adjudicators brought the very few captured Persian officers up to face the consequences of murdering so many of their kin living amongst the tribes of the steppes; all of their charges were punishable by death. It was a formality; the tribe's horsemen had committed to eradicating these overly proud intruders. Even the runner sent back to report to Xerxes was hunted down and immediately executed. Not a single Persian lip would ever whisper this story of defeat, and the people of the steps had no written language to tell them of the day; cinders and ash would be all that remained of these foreign invaders; the bone meal was too valuable to leave to rot on the surface so their bones and ashes would be ground together and spread on fallow grazing lands. Ultimately, no soldier in Hamedani's force would remain alive. Samid Al Sahan and Governor Hamedani were the last of Xerxes' henchmen to be brought into the makeshift tribunal. The men were bound with sticks and rope and looked as helpless as the many innocent people they had slain over their years of reigning terror, like all the wives and children who had fallen silent after witnessing or being subject to their perverse cruelty. Like every frightened child who was stolen and conscripted to serve as an unwilling soldier in his sad regiment, full of fear and wondering what fate awaited them, the balance they owed was fittingly deserved, inspired by all who perished at the barbaric hands of these defendants. The dark fit perfectly opposite the light, an act of quiet revenge for so many ghosts waiting for karma and equilibrium to make their injustices right again. These proud and powerful men would see the balance of their dues paid out exclusively by the manor of their demise, stoned to death by the very people that they exploited.

The burning of bodies continued for three days, as did the honoring of the gods. The cows injured in the battle were put down with the highest tribute paid. The witch supped with her kinsman at a table with no throne on which to rule. All the Tribes were amassed on the battle site in the Persian camp. They chanted incantations, drank concoctions of fungus and herbs, then trampled defiantly on this now hallowed soil. There would be no written words of this victory, only the pride in these men's hearts that brutal tyranny would always be eclipsed by the gleaming light of justice's shining beacon.

Days turned into weeks, and the gathering of the tribes of the Steppes finally came to an end. It was time to seek fall pastures and ready the herds for the winter's cold sting. Panothos thanked the old witch and the large chieftain, entrusting in their conspiracy to never mention the alliance's existence. Panothos was left with no gold for his troubles but was gifted many head of cattle and also many of their pelts to survive and prosper in their new lives in the northlands.

Ashkan was made a free man and allowed to continue to the Northlands. There was no way they would let him go back to Persia, but he didn't want to return to that dark existence in the first place. He knew there was no chance they would let him wander the earth with their secret, so he thought it best to remain in Panothos' care. He was hired as a servant to Gyttja, and his life was spared to Tyranos' dislike.

Finally, the procession packed up and moved northwest towards the cold lands again. After many weeks of traveling, Gyttja finally touched the crystal waters of her youth; her spirit glowed with her love for Panothos. Her belly protruded, swollen with his child. These new tribes and their new ways would surely test their mettle, and the

new gods would surely be just as absent as the old
and would rule ironically in absentia, only now from
a realm known as Valhalla.

Chapter 9

The Frozen Lands

When Panothos descended upon the land of the
North, he was enthralled by the wondrous sights.
Frozen mountains peeked at them from above; a
white fog was lying low and lingering in the bay.
Long boats with ornately carved dragons adorning
their bows were setting out into the mist; crews of
huge, long-haired men with braided beards coiled
ropes and pulled oars in unison. Nets hung from
masts, and each boat's sails were decorated with
colorful emblems and family crests. Gyttja was now
in the land of her birth; it was not her home but one
of many settlements that dotted the frozen
coastline. She could hear the men on the docks
yelling at one another in her native tongue.
Panothos could make out some of the words these
men were yelling; he even recognized some
phrases from listening to the girls speak to one
another. It was a strange new land of pale-skinned
giants. Even the women here were incredibly tall;
they dwarfed Gyttja and the other girls who had
survived the journey from Persepolis. The Spartans
marveled at the girl's height and natural beauty.
They had never imagined that women could be so
tall but beautifully proportional and pleasing to the

eyes. They looked as if they could snatch the men up and carry them away at will if they pleased. Aurias was taken aback by the tall beauties; they matched his stature, which he would never have imagined existed in the world.

In small stalls beside the pier, men smoked fish beside women who cleaned them and dumped their entrails into leaf-lined baskets. The waste parts of the animals would then be buried in the fields to grow food or used again as bait to catch more fish; nothing went to waste here. The frigid climate demanded total utilization of all the resources; unnecessary waste was viewed as criminal in this land, where starvation due to weather still occasionally occurred.

Panothos could feel the climate change in his bones; every injury he had ever sustained in the past left a pain that, at times, was breathtaking. He was not accustomed to the consistently cold weather, and his joints ached like he was being tortured again. Gyttja sat close to him in the saddle to try and keep his back warm. She massaged his shoulders to keep the stiffness from setting in. She asked Panothos to dismount as they approached the main building in the village, which was the long house of the village elder, the seat of power for the surrounding areas. Gyttja approached the guards who were posted at the entrance of the building; they were covered in bearskins and stood guard with massive battle axes at their side. She asked what the name of the leader of this village was. The men stood silently and stoically, but as she asked again, a large old man exited the massive structure through an ornately carved, solid wooden door. The man had a gray braided beard with crumbs of bread still lodged in its mats, obviously from the last meal he had eaten. He was escorted by two muscular women armed with sharpened staffs and adorned in gold-plated body armor. Gyttja, in her native tongue, asked the man if he was the leader of this village. The old man replied,

"I am ... I am Earl Ivan of Ribe, and who are you, my sweet girl?"

"I am Gyttja from Elslen; it is my honor to make your acquaintance, my lord," she replied.

The old man looked down his nose at her from atop the steps of the longhouse entrance and paused before he spoke or took another step.

"You cannot be from Elslen, my dear; the people of Elslen are now extinct for a whole generation; they befell a cursed blight. A great sickness that completely wiped them out over ten harvests ago. You speak our language; how don't you know this fact, child?"

"My Earl, I am truly from Elslen; I was sold into captivity many seasons before, so many now that I have lost count; I was just a young girl; I was rescued by these men with whom I now ride. We have traveled through deserts and across mountains for two seasons, battled the weather, and fought many foes to get here. I wish only to find my parents and return home to apologize for my absence."

"Ah, sweet Gyttja, you are as close to home as you will ever be again. Elslen has no life; it is the land of no mourned graves. Your parents, if they remained there, now sup with the gods. Any man who went there met their end from the great sickness."

"You may stay here in Ribe until the spring. But if you want to stay here in Ribe, you must pay tribute, and you may not go to Elslen and then return to us ... We do not want the ill will of the gods to send the sickness to our lands again." "What have you to say?"

Gyttja told Earl Ivan she would speak with her colleagues and return with an answer. A tear rolled down Gyttja's cheek as she walked back to the group ... never again would she hear her mother's voice or see her father's eyes. It sounded as if she was now all that was left of her family, like the Greeks ... forgotten orphans, cruelly sequestered by the whims of fate.

Panothos and the Greeks were huddled in the small stockyard next to the Earls' longhouse. The many head of cattle the Herdsmen had given them was all the wealth the group held, the only currency they had to barter with. Gyttja and Panothos discussed their options and agreed that an offering of some of the Bulls would have to suffice. Ribe was a fishing village and didn't have much in the way of livestock. The grazing land was limited to the summer melt, and during the winter months, when the night seemed never to end, livestock had to be held indoors to not freeze to death.

However, cattle were considered a scarce source of wealth, and they had no idea of the actual value the tribe of the north bestowed on them. Earl Ivan agreed to accept four of the herd, three cows, and one bull as tribute, which in these lands was a fortune. This offering would be sufficient to allow the group enough land to build a longhouse as soon as the spring's warmth descended. Panothos was grateful for Earl Ivan's peaceful offering of refuge. It would be nice to stop running and put down new roots finally. The journey had taken a lot out of them, but ever resilient, the Greeks began to draw up plans for settling the gifted land. They had enough head of cattle between them to farm, and many of the men possessed the skills to be master carpenters; some of the other men were fishermen in their former lives, so it would not be hard to assimilate into this new existence.

The season changed, and soon, they had cleared the ground for the new Longhouse; Aurias brought one of the finest bulls in the herd as an offering to the gods for blessings on this new life they now embraced. They butchered the animal and threw a feast for the entire village as a tribute for letting them make Ribe their home. The people of the village reciprocated when the men began to build the new longhouse. The locals offered their labor and expertise at every turn. Every board they raised together brought them mutual respect for one another; the combined knowledge and the skills each tribe shared and possessed were paramount to their collective long-term survival. The North men's knowledge of rope work and block and tackle impressed the Greeks. The mathematical drawings that the Greeks produced perplexed the North men, for all their knowledge was unwritten and passed down verbally. These new mathematical drawings were something they would absorb from the Greeks and use in future construction projects. Earl Ivan had generously allowed Gyttja a credit for some Pre-cut lumber from the mill. The Framing of the new longhouse was completed before the last morning frost finally cleared from the ground. Panothos and his men were to replenish the wood during the summer as agreed. For interest on the loan, they would teach some of the young men in the village these mathematical principles they had written and the tactics of professional warfare. The North men were strong, bold warriors, but they were more brawn over strategy; they could bully their way to dominance over an enemy with sheer audacity and blunt force but needed to try and test tactics when on the battlefield. Up till now, Ribe was only involved in localized skirmishes, but in the future, who knew what threats might impose themselves? When Earl Ivan saw the scars on their visitors, he knew that these men were not farmers or typical herdsmen. Once he saw the unified efforts of Panothos and his men to educate his people, he knew there would be much to learn about strategy and swords from these men. He welcomed their tutelage, reveling in their theoretical concepts and mastery of modern warfare. And so it was; a peaceful life had finally granted its mercy on Panothos and the group.

Over time, Panothos' beard grayed and grew long; he started to resemble his new neighbors in many respects. War ages a man much more quickly than the life of an average man. Gyttja braided his hair and kept him well.

By the spring melt, the hardworking Greeks had finished their dwellings, and most had become very fond of the Nordic girls. Some of the Greeks had even taken wives intending to start families. They were either far enough from the reach of Persia, or the empire had receded, and the men were now of no importance to Xerxes' maniacal ambitions; either way, they were free to enjoy this new way without fear of retribution.

Panothos and Gyttja welcomed a baby boy into their lives soon after arriving in Ribe. Since breaking with so much of his culture and traditions, he offered Gyttja to name the boy after Gyttja's father. In Spartan culture, the wife is a powerful equal, a pivotal force for the family, and a protector. In Nordic culture, it was mostly the same. She was pleased that Panothos thought of her in this light and would bestow such an honor unquestioningly upon her. Years of servitude had made her doubt her self-worth and strengths, but a man like Panothos nurtured her psyche, helped her overcome her fears and weaknesses, and gave her the confidence to be a strong, independent woman again.

Their child's name was Torbin, born a healthy child. He was a beautiful boy with dark hair, olive skin, and striking Baltic blue eyes. Torbin would not be raised as a Spartan or purely as a Northman ... instead, Panothos would take the best of both cultures and begin his own culture and traditions ... As with all traditions, they were considered unique initially, but as time progressed, these new ways would be endowed and carved in stone as rituals for future generations to embrace as a culture.

More and more seasons passed, Torbin grew, and the men built more houses and traded for large parcels of land spread all over the countryside surrounding Ribe. They absorbed the language and started building boats with the local woodsmen. They learned and shared shipbuilding techniques and wooden joinery. They became active in the local culture and seamlessly assimilated into the ways of their Nordic hosts.

Panothos had healed, but Gyttja could tell he was always in pain; she and Torbin did most of the chores so Panothos could begin advising Earl Ivan with his knowledge of statesmanship and military strategy. He apprised Earl Ivan with the knowledge of the unscrupulous character of some of the raiders they had come up against in their experiences, advising the earl to form a standing militia to protect Ribe from such hoards.

The earl was thankful for this information and paid Panothos for his services, appointing him to a council overseeing their defenses. Tyranos and Aurias were put in charge of the maintenance and training of the home guard because it was what they knew best. Neither the two of these men settled down with wives. They still acted like young soldiers who would find different girls in the drinking houses and would only seek temporary company with some of the tawdrier local women of the night.

They performed as Panothos asked and built a standing militia capable of being more than just a simple home guard; the men they trained for this force were massive and strong, and they looked carved of stone. They coupled the Spartan tactics with the Scandinavian blunt force approach and forged soldiers ready for anything coming their way on land or sea. They honed their skills as archers and learned battle formations like the phalanx. They took the men out on expeditions to raid the sworn enemies of Ribe; they quickly overran the untrained forces and undeniably dominated the region.

The men of Ribe were becoming known for their ferocity around the northern shores, spurring many young men in the region to volunteer to join their ranks. They became known for their toughness and brutality, becoming a legend to future generations. When the men overthrew a neighboring clan, they would offer them the option to join as allies or face annihilation. All Nordic men would be trained to seamlessly integrate into a more significant collective force and swear an oath.

As they conquered enemies, they gained control of trade routes, by which Earl Ivan accumulated great wealth. Once their forces had secured the ports of all their known enemies, Tyranos and Aurias reached a dilemma ... They were undeniably soldiers; they were forged only to be as such. Living a life of farming and fishing was not in them, and with no other enemies left to conquer, they thirsted for more. Once you have slain so many, it has been said, you hunger for that feeling. Once a warrior, always a warrior, and no man could deny this fact.

Panothos was in the back room of the longhouse, training Torbin to use a staff. Tyranos and Aurias approached, and Torbin ran to hug his uncles. Panothos told Torbin to go with his mother, asking his friends to sit and offered them a drink. The men accepted and then spoke privately in Greek to one another ...

"My dear friends, what has brought you to me today?"

Tyranos bowed his head. He had served with Panothos since they were teenagers, and the subject weighed heavily on his conscience. Aurias lifted his drink and toasted. The men drank and wiped the liquid from their long mustaches. Aurias began the conversation. "Panothos, my brother ... we come to you today with heavy hearts to ask your opinion." Panothos put down his bullhorn cup and, with a look of concern, asked, "What is it, my friends? What is it that bothers you on this day?"

"Sir, I will be simple and clear. We feel lost here ... we have secured the outer borders of Ribe and reinforced a defensive zone around these lands."

"We have tried to settle in and live as the North men do, but we are different … we are Spartans, and we still thirst to fight deserving foes."

Panothos interjected, "But you do fight our foes."

"You bring peace to this land through our perceived power."

"You have done great at what I have tasked you with."

"I understand, sir, but we are missing one critical thing, life's adventure … we seek life's adventure, and here in Ribe, we are just guards; we do not feel we are fulfilling our warrior destiny."

Panothos understood what his men were saying. He longed to do what he had been trained all his life. He also felt this strange draw, this need for danger, but his body was not strong enough to lead an army into battle. He had a child and a wife to ground him in this new life, so he discounted these feelings as immature longings. But he understood and did not argue with their desire. "Well, my friends, I understand completely." Tyranos raised his head and looked Panothos in the eyes, "So you feel this way, too?"

Panothos laughed. "Of course I do, but I must be pragmatic. My days of adventure are done, I am afraid … My bones hurt, but my heart is filled with the love of my family; they are now what I live for." Panothos poured another drink, which they knocked down in a shot.

Aurias and Tyranos understood Panothos' words; they would most likely feel this way if they were in his boots.

"So, what do you suppose you would like to do, my friends?" Panothos asked.

Tyranos spoke up first, "We wish to find our fortune in unknown lands and seek to join the gods on Mount Olympus in honor of our comrades who have fallen ..."

Panothos sighed ... He knew this day would come, and he feared the loss of his best friends and kinsman. He was now a domesticated and settled man; he would not leave Gyttja and Torbin. He left one life and began a new one; he did not want to abandon another.

"So, my friends, the day I knew would come has finally arrived ... we will feast in honor of your departure and future conquests before your departure!" Tyranos raised his head, and a tear ran down his cheek. He knew this would be the end of his time with Panothos. They poured another shot and toasted! They would never come so far to the north ever again. They craved adventure and the unknown. He deeply understood that dying in battle was the only way to enter the Pantheon.

"Thank you for your kind blessing, Panothos ... we shall make you proud, and we will tell the gods of your bravery and shrewd leadership."

Tyranos and Aurias were given war horses and ox carts; a few Greek Hoplites and Scandinavian men chose to accompany them with their wives. They, too, wanted to see the world and test their newly acquired skills. Earl Ivan called for the regents of the outlying villages to celebrate their departure with them in Ribe. The proud kingdom would be represented worldwide as its warriors followed the Greeks into whatever fate might show itself.

Two bulls were slaughtered, the strongest meads brought from the neighboring villages, in honor of their last feast before departing. The men jovially sang songs in the long hall, and the women joined the festivities. It would be a bittersweet departure, but Panothos was happy for his brothers; they would realize their potential and blaze their own trails. Toasts were raised, wonderful foods were eaten, and innocence was lost in the celebration that went late into the night.

In the early morning, as the kingdom slept and the sun began to rise in the distance over the vast North Sea, the small group embarked to the east. They had fine, newly forged weapons, freshly groomed horses, oxen, and a covered armored cart carrying all their supplies; they were a small expeditionary force of men tested in battle and trained to be the fiercest soldiers on the planet.

They would seek to battle the rumored "Keltoi" in the black forests of the south. The herdsmen told tales of these tribes, and the Greeks had also heard of the Black forests with Cannibals and men without languages or fear. They were the ancient humans, the ones who had come before. The ones who lacked the blessings of mighty Zeus or Freya and were closer in ancestry to the beast than to man.

Panothos arose early to see them off. He raised his sword into the air and let out a deep yell! Gyttja stood behind the door and watched the procession pass them; she grabbed his shoulders, laid her head on his chest, raised, and whispered in his ear ... "My love, I am again with child ..." Panothos lowered his head and kissed her forehead. She continued, "I am so lucky to have you as my man. I hope to raise our children to be visionaries like you!"

He replied, "No, my dear, I am truly the lucky one." They watched as the caravan moved slowly out of view and headed into the vast unknown. Deep in his heart, he felt they had finally earned their honor back.

Τελος

Written By:

Philip Andre Kay

Dedicated to

Dr. Mario C. Kay M.D.

And to my wife Jin Kay, who permits me the life and
space to create freely.

© 2024 ®